A NOVEL

SCREWED

xo, Toni ♡

TORRI HEAT

Cover Design by Books and Moods

Interior Formatting by Gee at DarkbyDesign

Editing by Lauren Alsten

Proofreading by Lauren at DarkbyDesign

Gotta make sure I'm going to Hell for a damn good reason.

Authors Note:
Please don't read this book if you have triggers with voyeurism, non-consensual/dubious consensual sex, rape, or sexual assault.

ONE

Mila

It didn't begin with a tornado, or a category five hurricane. There was no freak tsunami that destroyed half the eastern coast. No atomic bombs, leaving only destruction in their wake.

No. The beginning of the end was much more subtle.

The wheezing cough of a farmer, maybe two.

A bad season for corn.

Pregnancies ending abruptly with no reason.

All easily explained away. Until one day it wasn't.

Until one day someone noticed the disaster we were living in, and it became impossible to ignore. Too far gone to fix. We blamed it on global warming. On aliens. On each other.

At the end of the day, what caused our destruction didn't matter. We were too busy fighting for our lives at that point.

Half-full kindergarten classrooms and empty hospital wards – ghost towns of a time that seemed like only yesterday.

Our definitions changed faster than we could keep up with. Getting pregnant, next to impossible.

A live birth, a privilege.

Children themselves were defined as a commodity. Protected and cherished, but also used as currency in the strange new world we had found ourselves in.

And as with any form of currency, there were thieves and frauds. Black markets. Desperation.

Surprised? You shouldn't be.

Terrified? Not a strong enough word.

We were *screwed*, plain and simple.

It was still dark out when I began my day. It always was. My morning started before the birds sang their first note, and before the first ray of sunlight hit the horizon. There was too much to be done if I wanted to eat. Water had to be drawn from the old well a few miles away from my camp. A fire needed to be started, the water boiled, and food carefully rationed. Hunting, the bane of my existence.

This lifestyle was completely different from the one I had known before, but for now it was safer. At least until I figured out my next step.

It seemed like I was always figuring out my next step, but that system had kept me alive for the last ten years.

I pulled my worn sweatshirt over my head as a barrier against the morning chill and tied my once-white running shoes. Stepping out of my tent, I shivered.

Winter was coming far sooner than I liked, which meant I would eventually have to venture into a trading market, or worse, the city. My current sleeping bag wasn't warm enough to last through a freeze, and my toes were already going numb in my thin shoes. I had to risk it, for the sake of boots and a good sleeping bag.

I scrubbed my hand over my face, dirt sticking to my fingers. I should probably boil enough water to give myself a quick scrub. Sighing, I grabbed the bucket I used for water where it hung on a low tree branch. Everything was so much more difficult now. In the past, needing winter boots meant a quick trip to the mall, maybe an extra stop to grab a coffee or lunch.

Today, it meant I had to trek out of the woods, back toward civilization, and manage to stay out of the way of basically everyone. Standing out didn't help when you were trying to be inconspicuous. The city used to have a name, like all the rest. Emblazoned on signs, and used as puns for names of small bars. New York. Chicago. Los Angeles. But those names had evaporated along with everything else, dissolving with our morals. Arriving at the well, I drew a bucketful of water, careful not to spill any as I heaved it back up to the top. When I had fled the city, I hadn't known what I was doing.

Eventually, I realized I had to find a place that had all the resources I needed. I tried a bunch of different areas, but my current campsite was my favorite.

The woods that bordered an old farmhouse seemed like the best bet, and the well full of fresh water was a bonus. I didn't feel safe enough to stay in the house full time – and it felt weird to live in a house I was sure was filled with ghosts – but it reassured me to know it was there in case of a freak storm.

The city was a safe, one-day walk away. Far enough to be too much of a nuisance for the Kingsnakes to prowl, but close enough I could get there for supplies.

Avoiding exposed tree roots and rocks, I lugged my bucket of water back to the small clearing I used as my campsite. Winter was creeping in earlier than last year, and even earlier than the previous. Not like I should've been surprised. The pattern had been there for years.

We had just chosen to ignore it. We'd gone about our days, posting our lives on social media, drinking at bars and dancing at clubs, ignoring it all. The food shortages, and the longer winters. The decrease in birth rates.

It's funny, because at the time it seemed like a positive thing. Being able to have casual sex with less fear of getting pregnant? Sign me up.

Until people started selling their babies in exchange for food they couldn't find in stores. The fertile women had it easier, once they got over the idea of exchanging their babies for a liveable future. Because they had no babies to barter, the single men had it the worst.

Until the girls started disappearing. Friends of mine, or women I had gone to school with.

Whispers about a neighbor's missing daughter echoed through the near-empty grocery store. All twenty-something-year-old women, pretty, and hopefully viable.

Rumors swirled, talk of a black market that captured and impregnated young women. Once born, the babies were leveraged by the men for bartering. Because that's all they were at this point. A bargaining chip. An opportunity to claw your way to the surface.

I was not about to be treated like cattle, no better than a damn incubator. So when push came to shove, I ran. I found my clearing and my well, and set up camp. It wasn't much, but it was safe.

Using my light, I started a small fire with the kindling I had cut last night. It was half full, something else to add to the list of reasons I really needed to haul my ass to town.

Shit. I was hoping I'd be able to drag it out for a few more days, but I was crap at starting fires without my lighter, and the mornings were so damn cold. I couldn't afford to be without it for a day. I also really wasn't looking forward to losing my lighter.

Yeah, at the end of the day it was just a stupid lighter, but this one was special. This one brought back memories of *before*.

I rubbed my thumb over the long-gone Florida baseball logo – one that reminded me of spring breaks, sandy feet, and salty hair. A worn emblem of a team that no longer existed, and a city that no longer mattered.

My fire sparked, the dry wood catching flame quickly, but my half-empty lighter worried me. "You just have to be a big girl, Mila. Clean yourself up, get yourself to town, get your supplies, and get out. Easy." My voice was raspy, rough from a lack of use. I chewed a granola bar from my rations, waiting for my water to warm up so I could scrub the weeks of dirt off my skin.

The woods could be lonely sometimes, but it was better than the city. I could head south, toward an unofficial "trading market" set up by people like me – people who had fled the cities – but the chances they had what I needed was hit or miss.

No, it was better to risk the city, as much as I wanted to stay away. Lighters, a sleeping bag, and boots. And I really needed to grab a different flavor granola bar while I was there too. I was fucking sick of peanut butter.

With the water finally boiled, I dug up one of my cleaner washcloths, and stripped off my sweatshirt and long-sleeve shirt. It had been a while since my last "bath," but the effort it took to dry off in the cold didn't make it worth it often.

In the city, many people still had running water, and I would stand out with my grime-covered face.

I pulled my tangle of dark hair away from my face, tying it up with a bit of string I had fashioned into a ponytail. The hot water made me shiver in the damp morning, but it was still a pleasant feeling as I ran the cloth over my arms. I smiled, closing my eyes and imagining my hand was the gentle touch of a lover instead of my own, caressing my skin, pulling feelings out of my body I wasn't sure existed anymore...

Then I laughed, the sound bouncing off the trees that edged my clearing. The idea of me ever having a lover again was hilarious and improbable. Men wanted women for one thing, and one thing only, these days. A baby they could trade away. Running water, a roof over their head, and a warm meal made people do crazy things.

But I was alive, and I was free. I didn't need a man, or a woman, to deal with my sexual needs. Besides, sex wasn't exactly at the top of my list of priorities. Survival was number one, followed closely by food, and a good night's sleep.

"Get your head on straight," I muttered to myself. I needed to focus on my trip to the city, not think about sex. Satisfied with my cleanliness, I tossed my sweatshirt back on, and then stripped off my jeans. I scrubbed my legs until they were red, then threw my jeans back on.

I was fed, presentable, and ready for the dangers of the city. I hoped.

I stepped back inside my tent. Stacks of books lined the walls. The one good thing about the Collapse was all the time I had to read. I tried to sneak into the library whenever I could – when I felt safe. It wasn't often, but it was enough to satisfy my urge for words. I didn't care what I read. Fantasy, romance, self-help, self-defense... the only genre I avoided was dystopian. For good reason.

I grabbed my backpack, checked my water bottles to make sure they were still full, tossed in some granola bars, and counted my dwindling ripped dollars. Money only went so far these days.

Commodities went for much more.

The world had quickly switched to a system of trade, and unless I upped my hunting game, I had nothing to offer. The money would have to be enough. The thrift store might be my only option, but it was still better than nothing. I double-knotted my shoelaces, and set off through the forest.

The city was in the opposite direction from my abandoned farmhouse, so it was a longer walk in the woods than on roads, but I didn't mind.

The forest filled with evergreens gave me lots of places to hide if I came across people I didn't know. Unfortunately, this was the way my brain had to work now. Constantly thinking ahead, making sure I had a plan for everything. It was the only way to guarantee my freedom, and if I didn't have my independence, I had nothing. It helped that my survival skills weren't limited to knowing edible berries.

I could incapacitate someone, if I needed to. Even kill. My books helped me, and after the horrors I witnessed, you could never be too prepared.

The forest was quiet, even though it was late enough for the birds to be awake by now. Most of the wildlife had died off when we lost our major crops. It made my hunting difficult, to say the least. That's what I told myself anyway, again and again, when I failed to bring home a rabbit or a squirrel.

The morning shifted into afternoon, and I stopped to eat a granola bar. *Fucking peanut butter.* Even oatmeal would be better than peanut butter, day in and day out. On the other hand, I was lucky enough to be eating regularly. But still. Peanut butter?

I rolled my eyes and stuffed the empty wrapper back into my backpack – the world was enough of a disaster without my litter contributing to the problem. I continued my hike through the silent woods, my footfalls the only sound.

The sun began to sink, the light dimming in the forest. Just before nightfall, I hit the edge of land where the trees began to thin. *Perfect*. My timing gave me an opportunity to set up camp safely, and then continue into the city at first light.

I hummed quietly to myself as I looked around for a tree I could sleep in semi-comfortably. I didn't want to risk a hammock, not this close to the outside world. I needed to secure higher ground.

I wished Olivia was still here, someone I could laugh with about the absurdity of our situation.

Hunting scrawny squirrels, and sleeping in trees, when it seemed like only yesterday we had been laughing in our apartment, ordering pizza, and watching trash television. Olivia was my partner in crime, my best friend.

We had met as freshmen in university, two insecure girls with big laughs and bigger dreams. From that point on we were inseparable. Until Olivia was stolen in front of my eyes.

I settled into a tree with intertwining branches, giving me something to lean against as I slept. Not that it mattered. These days I slept with one eye open. I cushioned my head against my backpack, watching the last of the dying light fade out in the distance, leaving me alone with just myself and my thoughts.

It was almost as dangerous as the city.

The amount of people milling about the city was almost overwhelming.

Scratch that. It was entirely overwhelming.

You got used to being alone after a while.

People carrying on normal conversations, the same shops I had walked past countless times, they all assaulted my senses and made me want to turn and run. But I needed boots. A sleeping bag. *And a goddamn lighter.* I needed to work through it. I wouldn't be here for long.

"Excuse me! So sorry." A woman carrying a large purse stumbled into me, not paying attention to where she was going. Or maybe I had been frozen longer than I thought, watching the city wake up. I gave her a quick smile and stepped out of her way. Tugging my sleeves over my wrists, I took a closer look at her. She was definitely one of the lucky ones – the ones who could have babies, and had made peace with giving them up to stay alive.

Her hood was lined with fur, her plush coat a stark white in contrast to my dark clothes. I remembered when white clothes actually stayed white. Not anymore.

But thinking like that was dangerous, and I needed to stay in the here and now.

I shook myself off, walking in the direction of the department store I knew was only a few blocks away.

The city was surreal.

The occasional car still drove by, electric ones that only the richest could maintain. Fuel was nothing more than a dream. A lot of the stores couldn't keep up with the new way of trade and had gone under very quickly. That left the markets, which were hit or miss at best, and the department stores, which were so desperate to stay alive they would accept nearly anything as currency. It didn't mean the shelves were stocked, because they usually weren't. But it was better than nothing.

I walked past two women about my age. They whispered to each other as they strolled along the sidewalk. "Did you hear about..."

I couldn't quite catch the name, but her friend's reply was clear. "I heard she got snatched on the way to pick up her daughter from school."

The first woman responded with a cruel laugh, as if it had been her own fault for getting taken. As if women didn't deserve to have a safe place to walk, to live. As if we were no more than commodities ourselves.

I knew what I wanted from my life, and I knew it wasn't this. If I ever had a baby, I wanted that baby to be raised with love. I didn't want to live in *fear*. A man in a hoodie and a faded pair of jeans walked toward me, and I instinctively shrank into myself.

Don't draw attention to yourself. Rule number one.

It was easier to blend into the background. He passed me without a second look, and I sighed. The department store was within sight, the same neon sign lit up above the doors.

Except now posters covered the windows, a running list of things they no longer had in stock.

Some of the signs looked like they hadn't been changed in weeks, the tape peeling and the handwritten words faded from sunlight. I had a feeling milk wouldn't come in this Friday, and hadn't come in last Friday, or the Friday before that. I couldn't remember the last time I had milk. When the crops had died, the livestock had dwindled, unable to sustain themselves on the little left. Milk was rare, and beef was even rarer.

My breath came easier as I strode closer to the store. Stores were relatively safer than the streets. Not that clerks wouldn't look the other way, or couldn't be bribed, but again, it was relative.

Boots. Granola bars. Sleeping bag. Lighter.

I chanted my list as I stepped, the rhythm keeping my mind off the danger surrounding me.

Boots. Granola bars. Sleeping bag. Lighter. Batteries.

I hoped I had enough money. I could probably scrounge up a few tradeable things in the bottom of my backpack if I needed to.

Boots. Granola bars. Sleeping bag. Lighter. Batteries.

The store loomed thirty paces away. Funny no one was waiting outside. Last time I was here, there was a line to enter.

Boots. Granola bars. Sleeping bag. Lighter. Batteries.

Twenty steps away. One alley, but I could run past that if needed. I was basically safe at this point.

Boots. Granola bars. Sleeping bag. Lighter. Batteries.

The alley lurked on my right, but I kept my eyes focused on the store and picked up my pace.

I was so focused on the store and my chant I didn't notice the hand wrapping around my wrist until it was too late. I whipped my head from side to side, ready to scream for help, but I already knew the block was empty. A sweet-smelling rag was slapped across my nose and mouth, and then everything went black.

TWO
Ray

The first time the Kingsnakes had approached me, I was horrified. Kidnapping women, raping them, impregnating them against their will, and for what?

A better cut of beef? A warmer blanket?

The idea just didn't make sense in my head. I couldn't get the two pieces to fit together. I had declined them before they had even finished their sales pitch, which was perfected to be as smooth as possible.

Raised by a single mother along with my two younger sisters, I had always been taught to respect women.

Besides, I still had my job at the mill. It didn't make us rich by any means, but it was enough to keep food on the table, and the water running. Sometimes there was an extra bag of flour to sneak home, which was always a plus.

Life wasn't the same as it used to be, but my mom was past the age where she needed to be worried about being snatched, and my two sisters were still in grade school. It wasn't perfect, but we got by.

Avery. Ella.

I straightened my shoulders, my sisters' names echoing every step I took closer to the new captive.

Avery. Ella. Avery.

I was doing this for my sisters. *Ella. Avery.* I would provide for them. Protect them. Do what it took, at any cost.

Ella. Avery.

I trailed Luke into the common room, where a group of brothers stood in a semicircle around a young woman on her knees in front of them.

Ella. Avery.

The woman lifted her face to look at me, and I nearly tripped into Luke's back once more. My heart stopped. For a second, she looked an awful lot like a girl I had known before the Collapse. A girl who had stolen my soul. And then it beat again, thudding to life in my chest. Because there was no maybe about it.

Mila?

But you know the saying *bad things come in threes*? I saw it first-hand. Mom got sick, really sick, really quickly. We did everything we could, even got by on scraps for a week so we could afford a doctor. It didn't matter. I woke up early before my shift one morning to check on her, and she was gone. We were sad, but not surprised. That was the way the world worked now. The only thing to do was to move on.

Except then the mill shut down. The old farmer who employed me sighed when he told me there wasn't enough grain coming in to keep it running. He handed me an envelope with my last pay in it, slapped me on the back, and wished me well. I wasn't worried.

I could always find another job. I was young, able-bodied. Work would be easy to find.

The third bad thing left me desperate. Ella, my youngest sister, had fallen ill with the same thing my mom had. A deep cough that left her gasping for air, and a fever that she just couldn't shake. There was no money for the doctor this time, and I wasn't about to leave Avery alone to care for her.

So I had put my job search on hold, stretching the dollars of my dwindling pay envelope until I had no other choice. Ella, although still rough, was stable. I tucked her into bed, kissed Avery on the forehead with the command that she was to let no one inside except me, and stepped out into the dark night to find the Kingsnakes.

The girls were everything to me, down to the littlest detail about them, and I would do whatever it took to keep them safe. Ella still had her baby dimples, filling my nose with the smell of her strawberry shampoo whenever she walked into the room. Her dark hair was never brushed, and was even more of a tangle now that she was so ill. And Avery...

Avery with her bright blue eyes and blonde hair. I still saw a child when I looked at her, but I knew she was racing toward puberty faster than I would've liked. I'd have to hide her from the Kingsnakes sooner rather than later.

At least joining them would offer her some protection.

They weren't hard to find, if you knew where to look. The first member to approach me had been a guy I grew up with and used to play football with. If necessary, I could always find my way to the Kingsnakes through him. But it wasn't needed. They found me.

"Dawson." The voice calling my last name stopped me in my tracks. "You looking for us?"

I shifted uncomfortably from foot to foot. "Maybe."

The man stepped out of the darkness, the black hood of his sweatshirt obscuring most of his face in shadows. "If you're trying to play it cool, you really shouldn't look so obvious. Coming out after curfew is a stupid move."

"You're out here." The curfew was new – an attempt to keep the black markets and other seedy businesses somewhat in line. The only thing it did was make it easier for them to operate. The police had been useless since the last pay cut, and desperate people still went out at night. Now, I was one of those desperate people.

He shook his head, and I caught a glimpse of the bone mask that covered his eyes. It was the marking of a Kingsnake. Supposedly, it kept their identities hidden, but we all knew who was really behind the masks. "I have the protection of my brothers. What do you have to offer?"

I hesitated. This was a test, and I needed to pass. I needed to think of my sisters. The words didn't want to leave my mouth, a statement stuck on the tip of my tongue. A moment that would change everything. I could feel it in the air, and the way my stomach tightened. "Myself. I'm here to offer myself to the Kingsnakes."

The only acknowledgement I received was a tip of his head, before he turned and disappeared into the dirty shadows of the alley. I took a deep breath, looking around to make sure no one was watching my descent, and willingly stepped into the darkness.

My fall from grace, if you will, had been several months ago now. I was initiated into the brotherhood without much fanfare, or issues. Luke, my old buddy from football, had made sure my transition into the black market was seamless.

How easily one could go from a law-abiding citizen to a man who operated under the shadow of the moon still stunned me. I couldn't afford to be picky.

Not when they sliced my hand open with the rusted blade – a blood oath that made me a Kingsnake until my death.

Not when the resident artist tattooed the coiled Kingsnake across my heart.

Not even on the first night, watching the girl with sad eyes lie down on the bed in front of me. And especially not now, with Avery and Ella depending on me for everything.

The work wasn't hard, per se. We "operated" out of an abandoned motel on the edge of town. The electricity was long gone, and the key cards didn't work for shit.

But we had flashlights, and the old locks still worked just fine.

The remnants of visitors long gone still lingered – suitcases hastily tossed to one side, clothes scattered in various corners. For a while, after everyone realized the world was going to shit, the rich still tried to maintain a normal life.

They pretended to be happy, taking their families on vacation and acting like their useless titles weren't on the line.

CEO. Regional Director. President of Finances. They ignored food shortages, and the growing numbers of homeless on the street. But eventually the homeless grew desperate, the rich got mugged – or worse – and the vacations stopped.

We functioned much like a normal business would, before the Collapse. A normal, illicit business. There were about twenty-five or so Kingsnakes, an ever-fluctuating number. New guys would join us, only to disappear a week later.

We didn't ask where they went. We didn't need to.

Once you were in, you were in for life. Twenty-five guys, about as many girls, and two guns that didn't have bullets. No one could tell me the last time the guns had bullets in them. But the girls believed they had bullets, and that was what mattered.

I wasn't responsible for bringing the women in, thank God. I don't think I could've stomached that – snatching girls only a few years older than Ella from their homes and families, impervious to their cries. No, I was only responsible for the second half of the equation – if you could call it that. Young and hopefully fertile, I was on the "breeding line."

Once every two days, I would don my mask, and meet my young woman of the month in her room. By the time they got to the rooms, they were usually resigned to their fates.

Quiet, reserved. Willing, more often than not. Because what choice did they have? But still, it turned my stomach. I wanted to be better – better than my so-called "brothers" who were grateful just for a hole to shove their dicks into.

That kind of transaction had never sat well with me, even before the Collapse. I tried to separate what I was doing – *assault* – from what I needed to do – *feed my family*.

But the first night I was supposed to do my "job," I couldn't. I froze, imagining the girl's family. Her parents, waiting for her to come home. The future she should've had, away from the motel. And that very same night I made a decision. I wouldn't screw the girls.

Each month I would choose the girls I knew would keep my secret – or needed a break from one of the rougher brothers.

We would fake it the best we could, but it was still dangerous. If the other brothers found out I wasn't living up to the expectations of a fertile Kingsnake, it would mean certain trouble for me and my family.

Going against the blood oath meant death for me, and an even worse fate for my sisters. As for the girls... they knew the risk they were taking by sitting a month out.

Once I could trust them, I offered them some of my cut, allowing them to stockpile a small reserve of supplies in case they were able to escape. But I had to be careful. One slip of the tongue, and I was done for.

I couldn't let that happen, even if it meant my hands were a little less dirty of the sins committed here.

Like it made a difference. Each night I left home – pressing a kiss to my innocent sisters' foreheads, locking them safely behind the door – to come out to the motel, where a piece of my soul chipped away one evening at a time.

Maybe I wasn't committing such transgressions myself, but I was still standing by, allowing them to happen. A willing bystander. How long could I maintain this life before there was nothing left of me but bones cloaked in an artificial body?

But the payments, I thought. Because the payments were what kept me going. Hell, I was sure it kept most of the women going as well – a roof over their heads.

The Kingsnakes were, above all else, a brotherhood. And that meant we shared in the wealth.

A baby sold to a rich, aching woman meant food and supplies for all of us, divided up as equally as we could. It didn't matter who produced the babies, as long as we were all doing our part.

We knew who the others were, as much as we tried to ignore it.

We knew what brought us here, night after night. The men who went home to unsuspecting wives, crying softly in the shower as they washed away their sins.

A few of the others knew about my sisters, quietly slipping me an extra ration of bread, or a pair of shoes their own child had outgrown. And then there were the men who did it for themselves.

You could see the divide between the ones doing it because they had to, and the ones doing it because they could.

The ones who delighted in being the first to make a girl cry. They weren't here to feed a family, or to stay alive. They were here to feel *powerful*.

I stayed as far away from those guys as I could. But in the Kingsnakes, distance was always a problem.

I wandered the halls, climbing the stairs as the sun set. I tried to get to the motel before sundown on breeding nights.

The police weren't likely to mess with us, fearing for their own wives and daughters, but it was still easier to avoid conflict altogether. Upstairs was quiet.

I was one of the first brothers to arrive tonight, and even all of the girls' rooms were silent. The girls were probably asleep, or pretending to be asleep so the worst of the men wouldn't bother them until it was time.

I swung my mask around my wrist, sighing as I stopped in front of a window. Most of the front-facing windows were boarded up, helping maintain both our "secrecy" and our element of fear. But some windows on the second floor, facing the woods, were left open. The glass panels were long gone, sold or traded, nobody knew.

But still I leaned into the frame, dipping my head out into the fall night. The sun was setting, painting the forest across the way with hues of reds and yellows.

Ten years ago, you might have seen a deer darting into the trees. Not anymore. Any of the deer that had survived starvation had been hunted by desperate men.

Desperation made people do crazy things – even I knew this. I felt for deer watching their privileges of life slowly drain away.

Freedom was nothing more than a memory, an illusion that some tried too hard to cling to. We may not have the same rules and laws as we did before the Collapse, but freedom still wasn't a reality.

I still had to drag my feet to this motel, night after night. The girls in the rooms still had to put up with men using them as nothing more than incubators.

My sisters would never know what it felt like to step into the ocean, feeling the sand squish beneath their feet. They'd marry too young, if they were lucky. If not...

"Fuck." I gripped the wooden windowsill, the brittle splinters crumbling in my hand. This wasn't what I wanted from my life. Wasn't what I had expected. Hoped for. I turned away with a frown, finding my way to Hannah's room.

I knocked quietly, waiting for her soft, "Come in," before I entered. I had lucked out with Hannah. At the beginning of every month the girls lined up, and we selected our chosen female in an order similar to the now-nonexistent football drafts.

We would rotate girls in hopes it would increase our chances of impregnating them. And hopefully keeping them pregnant. Supposedly.

Whispers brewed around the newer members, telling a story of a woman who died in childbirth early on. Twins. None of them made it. After that, the next man recruited was a doctor.

He might've been a vet, but at the end of the day he kept the girls alive through pregnancy and that was all the other men cared about.

The members who had been with the Kingsnakes longer chose first. Rookies chose last. Those who had been lucky enough to impregnate a girl hovered somewhere in the middle. Unfortunately, those who chose first were usually the ones who mistreated the girls.

Power corrupted oh-so-easily in this new world of ours.

Tonight was the first of a new month, so we'd choose again. Hannah and I knew each other from when we were kids. It meant my arrangement was easily settled, because we had a quiet solidarity. I hoped whoever chose her next would be gentle with her.

She was a soft soul. Probably too soft for this harsh world. She reminded me of Ella, and I said a silent prayer to whoever was listening to spare Ella this life.

"Hey." Hannah offered me a smile, but her eyes betrayed her fear. She knew what tonight was. All the girls did. "You ready for tonight? I heard Laura was hoping you'd pick her..."

I rolled my eyes, and took a seat on the chair across from the sagging bed. The girls talked, when they could, and I was well aware of Laura's attraction to me. But someone actively hoping I would *breed* her was too much for me to imagine.

Not to mention, it would make my whole "don't screw the girls" plan unachievable. Laura would never let that slide, and I'd have my throat slit before I blinked.

If I was lucky.

"Laura will spend another month hoping then." I ran my hands through my hair, trying to put my thoughts into words. "I want you to be careful tonight. Don't stand out too much. I'll do my best to get one of the good brothers to choose you, but I can't guarantee anything, so just blend in as much as possible."

Hannah dipped her head in acknowledgement, a sheet of tangled red hair covering her face. "You gotta watch out for yourself too, Ray. If the brothers knew you were in here..." Her voice trailed off, but we both knew what she meant.

I'd be dead if the brothers knew I was fraternizing with a female for non-breeding purposes, or if they knew I wasn't actually fucking the girls I chose each month. And Hannah...

I didn't even want to think about what would happen to her. I got to my feet, brushing invisible dust off my shirt.

"I know. That's why I was never here." I gave her a smile, one I hoped was reassuring. "Good luck tonight."

Hannah pulled her frayed cardigan tight around her body. "You too. And I mean it. Be careful."

I gave her a quick nod, and stepped back out into the hallway. I'd kill for a cigarette. Or a drink. Hell, anything to do with my hands, to make me forget that this was the life I was now stuck in.

I pulled my mask up, the open windows letting me know the world was shifting further into darkness as I made my way downstairs toward the common room. Taking the steps two at a time, I almost ran directly into Luke. Luke steadied me, holding me at arm's length so I didn't take both of us down.

"Brother, I was just coming to find you. What were you doing upstairs anyways?"

I froze, trying to think on my feet, which was unfortunately not my strong suit. "I thought I heard one of the girls screaming. Came up to see what all the fuss was about."

Luke shook his head. "Damn females. They're lucky we keep them locked away up there. Who knows what kind of trouble they'd cause out on the streets."

I realized too late into my initiation that Luke was one of the original Kingsnakes. The ones who thrived on the power, the control. I learned to cloak my emotions around him, school my reactions so he'd think I was one of them.

"Definitely." But his opinion of the young women upstairs turned my stomach.

"No matter. Come on downstairs. One of the young guys brought us some fresh meat. He tried to claim her for himself this month, but I thought you deserved a turn with one of the new ones." He turned and started down the stairs. With no choice, I followed, my heart sinking with every step.

Could I be the first to ruin a girl's life? To take away the little hope and freedom she thought she had left? What the hell was I doing here?

THREE
Mila

Coming back to consciousness was like waking from a heavy dream. The ones you couldn't be certain if they were real or fake. My head was foggy, thick with confusion, and blinking my eyes open took actual effort.

What the hell, I thought. I must have dozed off longer than expected after my trip to the city. My trip to get supplies... supplies I couldn't remember getting.

Because I never got the supplies.

My eyes immediately flew open. *Shit.*

I never got the supplies because I had been pulled back into the alley. And I knew exactly who had taken me.

Kingsnakes.

I moved my heavy head from side to side, taking in my surroundings. I was alone, thank God for that. My wrists were bound behind me, rope scratching into my skin.

My backpack was nowhere in sight, but I could feel something against my thigh in one of my more discreet pockets. I made a mental note to figure out what it was, later.

The room they had left me in looked like what was once the front desk for a motel – and not a nice one.

The windows were boarded up, and the door was heavily padlocked. I guessed my captors didn't use that entrance for anything. I closed my eyes, taking in a deep breath.

Was this my worst nightmare? Absolutely.

But I had survived for too long to let this be my downfall. I just needed to act dumb, and get my ass out of here. Guys used to like dumb girls. It made things easier for them. Surely some still did, even after the Collapse.

Behind the splintered desk, an open door revealed what looked like it had once been an office, but it seemed empty now.

From behind another door I could hear whispers. Men, waiting for me, to what, wake up and let them have their way? I didn't know what to expect, but whoever these men were, they definitely weren't expecting me. They'd be damn sorry they ever snatched Mila Spencer off the streets.

As if they could hear my thoughts, feel the fury flooding my veins, the door swung open, crashing into the wall.

A man of average height stood in the doorway, crossing his arms. He wore a black hoodie, the light just barely illuminating the edges of the bone mask covering his eyes. "Get up, female. And save your tears for later. I hate it when they fucking cry." I narrowed my eyes, biting my tongue to stop myself from making things worse.

28

Play dumb, Mila. Play dumb and you might survive this.

I had never craved my tent in the woods as badly as I did at this moment. My small fire pit, the sounds of the forest around me.

This room was too artificial, our interactions nothing but children playing pretend in a twisted fairy tale.

I wanted to go back to reality. But I needed to survive in order to do that. So I softened my face, selecting an expression of confusion as I stumbled awkwardly to my feet. "Who... who are you? Where am I?"

I knew who he was. I knew where I was. But I wanted to hear him say it. Wanted to watch his cruel mouth shape the words that would seal my current fate. He curled his thin lips into a smirk, openly checking me out as I walked toward him.

The door closed behind us, and he gripped my shoulder as we walked down a narrow hallway, passing an overturned ice machine.

"You're here to serve your purpose. If you're lucky, your belly will swell with a child we can profit from. And if I'm lucky, I'll be the one to put it there. After all, I did bring you in. Seems only fair." He yanked me backward, turning me to face him.

I couldn't make out his facial features, but his leer only emphasized it had been a while since he had laid his hands on a toothbrush.

Please, don't let him be lucky, I begged silently, trying not to gag. *Or me for that matter.*

He rubbed a grubby thumb across my cheek.

"You're definitely one of the prettiest we've brought here in a long time. Not used up like the other ones. A little dirty, but I don't mind a bit of grime." He smiled, openly displaying pale gums with several missing teeth. "I bet you'd even enjoy it." He leaned in closer, holding me still with his hand, and I realized he was going to try and kiss me with that disgusting mouth.

I could knee him in the crotch. Or I could headbutt him once he got close enough. Neither of these screamed "dumb female" though, and I didn't want to die ten minutes in.

His rancid breath inched closer, and I forced myself not to react. It was just a kiss. Just one kiss. Worse would come later, but I could deal with a kiss. I wouldn't throw up. Wouldn't react. Wouldn't...

"What do you think you're doing, Brother Dogberry?" A commanding voice forced my captor to jump away from me, even as his grip on my shoulder tightened. "You were supposed to be finding out her name."

"Nothing, brother. The female was acting out, and I was just making sure she knew her place." He squeezed his hand, but his foot tapped on the floor beside me. "And her backpack says Mila in permanent marker, so I'm guessing that's her name."

Interesting. I didn't like the way my name filled his mouth, but I filed this piece of information away for later. Seemed not only was there still a hierarchy in the black market, but the "brothers" weren't supposed to touch a woman without permission. I could definitely use that to my advantage. Also... Dogberry?

30

Just what kind of messed up cult had I stumbled into?

The other man in the black hoodie and mask rolled his eyes. "Whatever. Just bring *Mila* in here. The Choosing will start soon, and our brothers are interested in meeting the new recruit."

I stifled a laugh. Somehow I didn't think Dogberry was going to get first dibs on anything, even if that happened to be me. I focused on my breath as we walked to keep my wits about me. We followed the larger man through the doorway into what appeared to be an ancient breakfast room.

Old wooden paneling and wallpaper lined the walls, and where this had peeled away, newspapers acted as makeshift decorations. One boasted the local baseball team's win.

Another announced a holiday parade. I had stayed at motels like this, minus the newspaper decorations, before the Collapse.

Before the world went to shit, when I was just a college kid with nothing more to worry about than my exam the next week, or sleeping through a class.

Olivia and I would rent rooms as we road tripped down to Florida, cheap and convenient. Predictably someone would pull a bottle of cheap vodka out of their bag, and we'd spend the night getting wasted, rolling out of bed in the morning just in time to catch the last round of free breakfast.

Damn, I could almost smell the waffles in the air now, even though it had to have been at least a decade since this motel had a functioning waffle iron. A sharp kick to the back of my knees brought me out of my daydream, sinking me to the floor instead.

"Brother Brutus asked you a question, female," Dogberry spat. *Dogberry. Brutus.*

Where had I heard those names before?

I tried to center my anger, keeping a dumb expression on my face. But when I got out of here, he would be the first person I would take down. The asshole with the bad teeth, thinking he could get away with calling me *female.* "I'm sorry. I wasn't paying attention."

I remained on my knees, leaning only my head up to look at the small group of men surrounding me.

They all wore black hoodies, their identities "hidden" by the bone masks they wore. It wouldn't keep them hidden if I saw them individually, but in a group they all blended into the next. One of the men stepped forward, and my captor finally released his grip on my shoulder.

This guy, *Brother Brutus*, must be one of the ones in charge, judging by the way all the other men innately turned toward him. "I asked you if you knew why you were here," Brutus repeated, approaching to crouch in front of me. "Do you know what will be expected of you?"

He made sure he was eye level with me, but I knew the game he was playing. He was trying to put me at ease, get my guard down. But I didn't miss the ice piercing his blue gaze. This man was not here to be my friend. I looked up at him through my lashes. Demure. Pure. Malleable. All the things he expected me to be. "I'm here to serve my purpose."

The man nodded. "Precisely. You are here because you have been chosen. It's an honor, really. Each month, one of my brothers will select you in what we call the Choosing.

32

He will come to you every other night, for what we call the Ceremony, until you are pregnant with his child. If it doesn't happen that month, the next month another brother will take a turn. And so on and so forth." He slid a knuckle under my chin, forcing my head higher just to stare me down. "You *will* bear us a child. The world has no purpose for useless women any longer."

A *Ceremony* to produce a *child*. Put two and two together, and it wasn't difficult to know what he meant.

Rape. Forced breeding. I wanted to gag.

But even if I ignored his choice of words, I didn't miss the threat lacing them. There would be no leaving this place alive unless I escaped. "I'll do my best, sir." The title stuck in my throat, but I coughed it out, knowing it would add credibility to the part I was playing.

Sure enough, he gave me a smirk, releasing my chin. "Good girl. You'll fit right in here. Now, you'll attend tonight's Choosing as a formality, but Brother Prospero here will be taking you for himself this month. An honor for both of you." He leaned back, tipping his chin toward a tall man standing coolly to the side.

Behind me, Dogberry began to complain, only to shut up with one scathing glare from Brutus.

Shakespeare, I thought. Their names were taken from Shakespeare. It seemed like so long ago I had opened those dusty books, sitting in a classroom. Another life.

I eyed *Prospero* warily. I didn't want to be here. I didn't want to be in this situation. The idea of this man's – of any man's – hands on me made me sick to my stomach...

33

But I had survived this long thanks to wit, and I knew there was no way out of one night of hell. I could just make out a bit of a dirty-blond curl touching his shoulder underneath his hood. I wanted to scream. I wanted to retch.

I wanted to run back to the woods, turn back time, and tell myself not to go into town. To suck it up and go to a market instead. But I was here now.

I couldn't change the past. I could only move forward. And if Olivia had somehow survived a place like this, I could survive it too. For her.

Fuck. Is this what Olivia felt when they took her? This overwhelming combination of fear and sickness, a lack of control so deep it felt like you'd never unspiral completely?

Olivia. This was my penance for running, for leaving her behind. No question about it. But really, what else was I supposed to do? I would've still ended up here, just far earlier, and far less prepared.

"Pay attention!" Dogberry snapped, kneeing me sharply in the back. Shit, that hurt. I was half a second away from whirling around and snapping at him, but Brutus took care of it before I could.

"Cooper!" he snarled. "Know your place."

Cooper. Cooper was my kidnapper's real name.

Not *Dogberry.* And Cooper would be the first to die.

From what I had seen, the brothers were careful to only use their Shakespearean names around me, but Cooper must have already been toeing a line.

Brutus offered me a hand, pulling me to my feet.

"You'll have to excuse him. He's still young. I asked if you were ready for the Choosing. You will be chosen first, of course, and my brother will show you what is required of you from there. Do you accept this honor?"

I realized he was asking me if I accepted. If I accepted being assaulted and raped, impregnated against my will, only for my child to be sold. He acted like all of this was some kind of blessing for me.

Was he seriously this delusional, or was something else going on here? Regardless, I knew I had to play dumb. Not necessarily act like I wanted it – they wouldn't buy that.

But at the very least, I would have to seem dense enough that they could control me. I pressed my lips together, nodding. This seemed to appease the Kingsnake, and he turned around to Prospero with the longish blond hair. "And you, my brother? Do you accept this honor?"

"I do," was his curt, gruff reply. Something in my brain snapped to attention, a memory falling into place. I knew that voice. Or a voice like it. Because the man I had known in university wouldn't be here. He wouldn't have hurt a fly, let alone take a woman against her will.

But I couldn't shake the memory of his voice, running over me, flooding my veins with euphoria. His low timbre, whispering how much he loved me as we lay in bed, holding each other in the gray dawn. The way his gravelly laugh would make my heart hurt. But I was here, and the man that was supposedly "claiming" me for a month couldn't be Ray. I had left Ray in the past, along with cheap motels, vodka, beach trips, and Olivia.

In front of me, the Kingsnake's tanned face split into a smile. "Splendid. Round up the rest of the females. It's time for the Choosing." Several of the men made their way up the stairs at the opposite end of the room, while the one I assumed was the leader brought me to stand against the peeling wall. Surely once, it had been white. Clean and bare. Now it was dirty and scuffed, more ash than snow.

All of these titles they had for such vile acts made it seem so official. Because how could rape be rape if it was a *Ceremony*?

How could an auction be an auction if it was the *Choosing*?

I wanted to be sick all over blue-eyes' sneakers. But it was my own damn fault. I had been careless for all of twenty seconds, and now I was paying for my mistakes.

One by one girls shuffled down the stairs, some dressed in sweatpants and jeans. Others were barefoot, some wore heels and dresses.

It was apparent which of the girls didn't mind this supposed *honor*, and which girls were ready to bolt at the first opportunity. I didn't think I knew any of them, but that didn't mean anything. Surely an extended length of time in this place would change anyone beyond recognition.

Next to me, a girl teetered in heels like ones I used to wear to the bars – glossy, black, and out of place in our surroundings. Her hair was a mess, but I could still see the time she had taken to make herself look presentable. She must have been stunning once, the kind of girl who drew attention wherever she went. She glanced at me out of the corner of her eye. "Hey, new girl. What's your name?"

She spoke so quietly, I almost missed it. I kept my eyes forward as I whispered back, "Mila."

"I'm Laura." She laughed, a raspy noise that sounded more like a cough. "Welcome to hell, Mila."

FOUR

Ray

Surely it couldn't be her. There was no way the Mila I knew would be careless enough to get herself captured. Of course, there was no doubt in my mind she'd still be alive – Mila had always been feisty and full of fire. The Collapse wouldn't have stopped her from thriving however she could. But to be here, with the Kingsnakes? *No.*

But when she lifted her face to look up at Luke, I knew it was her. There was no mistaking those blazing emerald eyes, even from her submissive position. Her expressions warred for dominance across her freckled face, attempting to remain in control. I knew that look all too well. The look that screamed "just you fucking wait." I was certain no one else could pick up the minutiae of her emotions like I could, watching as she relaxed into a blank mask.

Because you couldn't look at the love of your life, the one who got away, and *not* know exactly what she was thinking at any given moment.

My blood ran cold when I realized Luke wanted me to break Mila in. First problem, you couldn't break Mila. She would break you, shatter your heart into a thousand pieces with no remorse, then toss you a broom so you could clean up your own mess. I wasn't sure my duct-taped soul could handle that another time.

Second, and bigger problem? We weren't supposed to have relationships outside of breeding with the females. I wore my mask, true, and I probably looked different than the Ray she knew in university, but she would still recognize me the minute we were alone together. I wasn't sure how long we'd be able to keep our past a secret from the Kingsnakes, which would be dangerous for both of us. And I had my sisters to think of as well.

Dammit. The shock of seeing Mila had made me forget what was most at stake here. Two young, innocent lives who didn't deserve the fallout of whatever consequences awaited all of us if this came out.

I had two options. Suck it up, and hope Mila and I could pretend like nothing was out of the ordinary, or corner Luke before the Choosing and demand someone else take Mila this month. Make up some bullshit reason. She had hurt me, broken my heart. But I needed to keep her safe. She wouldn't just end up with a broken heart, the Kingsnakes would try and break her *soul*. I couldn't have that on my conscience. I so badly wanted to corner her and demand answers, but...

I could see my baby sister's innocent face if I were caught, screaming as they took her away from me. I knew what I needed to do. Option two. It was safer for all the parties involved, no matter how badly my heart longed to reach out and touch her tanned skin.

So I watched from a distance as Cooper, the asshole he was, pushed Mila around. Luke had slipped up and used his real name, so I would do the same. He didn't deserve the protection of our other names. Not that his – Dogberry – was much better.

My anger demanded blood, but I couldn't give in. Instead, I silently crossed my arms when Mila agreed to be *mine* for the month – as if Mila could ever be owned by anyone. I said the words required of me, the vows tasting like pennies in my mouth.

And when Mila was lined up against the wall, expression still dull, I pulled Luke to one side. The other girls passed silently by us as we stood behind the ancient bar. "Choose someone else, Luke," I choked out.

He raised an eyebrow at me, and I was unsure if he was more surprised at the command in my voice, or my request. "You don't want the first turn with the new girl? I thought it would've been an honor for you. A show of my respect."

"Believe me, I am honored. But I don't think I'm ready to be a first yet. I just don't think I have what it takes." I couldn't push too hard, let my real emotions slip past. I had to protect my own interests, and Mila too.

Luke narrowed his eyes at me, trying to figure out my game.

"You sure? Cooper seemed eager to take her for himself, but I thought a pretty thing like that deserved a real Kingsnake for her first. I wanted you to be that man. But if you're certain..." He turned away from me, and in the space of no more than a second, I realized what I truly had fucking gotten myself into.

What would be worse for Mila? Having to hide her past with me, or being bred under Cooper's rough hands? We all knew what he was like. We saw the bruises on his girls of the month, the red marks they tried to hide with cardigans full of holes. Could I really sacrifice Mila to such a brute?

"Wait."

Luke turned back around, victory blazing in his eyes. I knew why he wanted me to be first. He wanted me to be more integrated into the Kingsnakes, wanted me to take more of a leadership role, and so far I had done my best to stay back.

Luke knew how much I despised Cooper. He also knew I wouldn't let a girl fall into his hands at my doing. But my taking the first turn would change things, and we both knew it. I closed my eyes, muttering a silent prayer. "I'll do it."

"Good man." Luke smiled and clapped me on my shoulder, but his grin didn't quite meet his icy blue eyes. "Now let's get these girls chosen."

We joined the rest of our brothers, watching the girls as they arranged themselves along the back wall. It had been awhile since our last new girl, so most of them knew what to expect. We had eighteen girls in total – nineteen now with Mila – another three were pregnant. They were kept in a separate part of the motel.

Luke didn't like how emotional the other girls got when they saw the swollen stomachs. I was happy to see Hannah doing her best to blend in with the wall.

But my face was on fire, and when I turned to see Mila standing at the end of the line I knew it was her angry gaze that was boring holes through my skin.

Every inch of her body screamed revenge, so at odds with Laura's attempt at sensuality next to her. Laura offered me a small wave, and I did my best not to shudder. How anyone could enjoy this life was beyond me.

Luke began with his normal opening, and I tuned him out. Drew, the Kingsnake next to me, bumped my shoulder. "Hey man, lucky you getting first dibs on the new hottie."

I clenched my fist, digging my fingernails into my palm. I liked Drew, I really did. He wasn't the worst of the Kingsnakes, but not someone I'd call a friend necessarily either. But I didn't want him talking about Mila like that. She deserved better. "Yeah. Lucky me."

I pulled my hood further over my face and inspected Mila more closely. She was older than the last time I had seen her, obviously. We had barely been older than kids back then.

But there was no doubt she was still just as beautiful. Her brown hair tangled around her face, her skin, tanned and smooth.

Wherever she had been hiding out, she spent a lot of time outside. Freckles dotted her nose and cheeks, calling me back to an afternoon spent in the sun kissing every single one of those freckles, reiterating how much I loved her with each kiss. She laughed and blushed, but I refused to stop.

Back when life was simple, and easy. When we could dream of more than just surviving through to the next day.

Somehow I had drowned out most of Luke's speech, not surprising considering it varied little from month to month. Next thing I knew, he called my name, and I shook myself back to reality. "Brother Prospero, you're first to choose."

I fucking hated my name. Luke thought it was fitting and ironic, but all it did was remind me that I controlled these women.

I'd rather think about the end of *The Tempest*, when Prospero renounced magic instead. When he found true freedom. I swallowed the hatred of my name long enough to step forward, ready to play the part of a dutiful Kingsnake.

The girls stilled, knowing what would come next. Laura looked up at me with eager eyes, adjusting her dirty dress to show more cleavage. I wanted to cover her up and send her home. She didn't deserve this. None of them did.

I looked Mila dead in the eyes, daring her to recognize me, to see through the mask I wore. But she only looked past me, through me, already compartmentalizing. She did that so well. Or she used to. I stuffed down the memories. "This month, for the honor of bearing my child, I choose... Mila."

Laura gasped, shooting Mila the dirtiest glare I had ever seen the woman use. Obviously she wasn't all about being demure and malleable, at least not when it came to the other girls. Mila's gaze didn't shift from whatever she was staring at over my shoulder.

If I knew her as well as I hoped I did, I would put money on the fact she was plotting something.

I tore my eyes away from her long enough to see Luke offer me a proud smile. I didn't want his pride. I didn't want anything he offered me.

But desperate times called for desperate measures, and I could no longer afford the luxury of being choosy. I tipped my head down in a slight acknowledgement of respect, repressing the anger brewing beneath my skin.

Luke turned back toward the girls. "Mila. I hope you understand the honor we are offering you. A place to belong. An opportunity to thrive, even when the darkness encourages us to fall. I hope your fertility serves you well, and you bear us a healthy child, and thus are able to provide the family with plenty. Together, we will rise."

His short speech was common for the new girls, usually changed up by a word or two, but tonight it made me want to gag.

Together, yeah fucking right.

Luke might feel like his sins were washed away by providing the girls a roof over their heads and food in their bellies in exchange for their babies, but at the end of the day they were still captives.

Taken from their families, their lives, against their wills. We all had been really. Safety was an illusion, and the Kingsnakes fancied themselves the magicians pulling rabbits out of hats.

I walked toward Mila, who still refused to meet my eyes. I grabbed her wrist firmly, and pulled her behind me toward the stairwell, leaving the next brother in line to choose his girl.

She followed me without complaint or resistance, which terrified me. Either she had entirely lost her will to fight, or she was planning to slit my throat the second she got me alone – honestly, I didn't know which one I preferred.

Her footsteps echoed mine as we walked the worn floorboards of the second floor, toward the end of the hall where I knew there was an empty room. I dragged her into the room behind me, closing the door with a soft click.

Once we were alone, her demeanor changed entirely.

She spun around the room, taking in her surroundings, before turning to face me with one eyebrow raised. This time, she at least looked at me, even if it wasn't directly in my eyes. I'd take it, especially after a decade of nothing from her.

The heat of her angry stare, the discerning gaze she ran over my body... damn, it felt good to be in her presence once more. I could hardly believe ten years had passed.

"So," she began, hands on her hips. "How does this whole breeding thing work? Are you really expecting me to just roll over and play dead while you do your thing?"

I stayed silent and took her in. The quiet fight, rising up as she gained steam. The snarky response, disguising fear with attitude.

"Well?" Mila narrowed her eyes. She turned and sat on the edge of the bed, bouncing up and down a few times as if to test the quality of the mattress. I watched her carefully, not able to get enough of her. Immediately she scowled. "Please tell me you're not one of those guys who gets off on women fighting and screaming. I don't play well, and you'll end up with a concussion before you even get your pants unzipped."

I couldn't do this any longer. It was too hard, my heart beating too rapidly. I needed to rip off the bandage and tell her who I was – consequences be damned. And this tough front of hers... God, it hurt my heart. "Mila, drop the damn act."

"Who are you to tell me what to do? You fucking kidnapped me. I think that basically invalidates any opinion you have." She smirked, but I saw the wariness behind her eyes. "Although it's funny. You do remind me of someone I used to know, before the Collapse. He thought he could tell me what to do too."

Did I think I could tell her what to do? Fuck no. I wasn't stupid enough to think I could control Mila. But I couldn't lie, I had probably tried. I was young and stupid and desperate.

Now I was older, slightly less stupid, and ten times more desperate. I dropped to my knees in front of her, and she recoiled ever so slightly. "I need you to promise me you won't scream. I don't want to gag you, but I will if I have to."

Mila scowled. "If you think I'm not going to scream as I'm fucking being *bred*, then you have another thing coming."

I closed my eyes, willing my heartbeat to steady.

She doesn't know, I reminded myself.

She's still in the dark.

"I'm not breeding you. I just need your word."

"Fine." Mila rolled her eyes, tossing her hands out to the side. "If Brother Prospero wants me to promise not to scream, then I promise to keep my mouth shut."

My heart tightened. "Don't call me that."

46

"What should I call you then?" she snapped. "Kidnapper? Cult leader? Insa–" Her words immediately cut off and her eyes widened as I pulled my hood down and tugged the face mask off. When she spoke again, it was little more than a whisper. "Ray?"

I didn't respond, waiting for it to sink in. A beat of silence passed, and then another.

She opened her mouth, and I wasn't sure if she was going to scream at me, or tell me she loved me. "Holy shit, Ray. It really *is* you."

I knew the emotions running through her were the same ones I had earlier in the evening. A ghost had been brought back to life, and now here we stood in the flesh in front of each other.

FIVE

Mila

Whatever they had knocked me out with had to still be in my system. I must have been delusional, hallucinating, *something,* because surely my sweet, protective boyfriend from university couldn't have been there.

But there was no disguising the guilt that flooded his gray eyes, and the dirty-blond hair that curled down to his shoulders. He had kept his hair shorter when we were younger, tidy. I shouldn't expect him to look the same, because only hell knew I looked completely different from the girl he had fallen in love with. But I couldn't juxtapose the Ray I used to know, who smiled at me from across campus, and picked me up at my dorm with flowers, with this man on his knees in front of me.

"What the fuck are you doing here?" His jaw tightened, the muscle ticking beneath the skin.

"What are any of us doing? What we have to do."

I scoffed. We all had to do things we didn't want to do in this world, but there was always a choice. I had chosen to live alone in the woods. Ray had chosen to assault innocent women and sell their babies. "And what you have to do is stick your dick in unwilling women?"

"No." His response was firm, and his eyes didn't waver from mine. Was he so brainwashed that he truly believed what he was doing was right? My stomach churned unhappily, and I was immediately grateful I couldn't remember the last time I had eaten.

I saw red, my blood pumping furiously. I couldn't control the anger I had toward the man I thought I knew. The man I once thought I would marry. "What do you mean, no? These women aren't your girlfriends, Ray. This isn't the fucking *Bachelor*. I'm not stupid. I know what the Kingsnakes do, and I know why they kidnapped me. I know what you're doing. You can tell yourself whatever you want so you can sleep at night, but I'll call it as I know it. *Rape*." I looked away from him in disgust, but there wasn't much else to look at in the barren room.

Ray grabbed my chin in his hand – one of the same hands I remembered running down my body in the still of the night – and wrenched my face to look at him again. His eyes were deadly serious, even more so than that night so long ago. "Mila. Shut up for five seconds and listen to me. I don't rape the women."

I narrowed my eyes. "And I'm a friggin' supermodel. The whole Choosing and bone mask tell a different story."

"I don't rape them." Ray released my chin, and I felt an odd sense of loss from where his hand had gripped me so tightly. Sitting back on his heels, he ran his hand through his tangle of curls, a motion I remembered well. I waited to hear what excuse he was going to pull out. "Each month, I choose a woman who will keep my secret. Every two nights, I pretend to fuck them. But I don't touch them. In exchange for their silence, I offer them a portion of my payments. And now I'll need you to keep my secret as well. If it gets out that I'm going against the blood oath..." He trailed off.

I shook my head, only slightly less angry. "You're still here, knowing what they do every night to these girls. What they want to do to me. How do you make your peace with it? Do you even think about their families? Fuck, Ray, do you even think about *Avery*?"

"Goddamit, I'm only here *because* of Avery," he roared. He pushed up off his knees and rose to his feet. He turned away from me, and even though I could no longer see his face, I could feel the thrum of anger as it stretched between us. "I'm thinking of Avery every single night. Avery, and Ella, too. I'm thinking about how I don't want them to end up here, or on the streets, or starving, or a thousand other possibilities that are way too *real*. So yeah, I come here and sell my soul. And try to make it a little less dirty. But I'm only doing it because I have no other fucking choice."

Ella? Who was Ella? "There's always a choice," I muttered. He didn't bother turning around to look at me.

"Real sound logic, coming from the girl who ran off the moment things got rough."

"Excuse me?" I clenched my hands into fists, my heart racing. I tried to remind myself that he didn't know about Olivia. How could he? But I was indignant and I couldn't stop the words from spewing out. "Did you want me to sit still while the world fell to shit around us? When tomorrow couldn't be guaranteed, let alone next week?"

"I looked for you, you know. I went to look for you the next morning, but your apartment was nothing more than a burnt-out shell. It was still hot to the touch." He shook his head, his words so quiet I wasn't sure if they were meant for me. But then Ray whirled around, glaring. "I told you I would fucking protect you. I promised you the world that day, Mila. I promised I would shelter you with my life. And instead you just never showed up the next morning. In fact, you never showed up... *ever*."

I jumped to my feet, forcing myself to ignore the electricity pulsing between our bodies. What was once there couldn't still be. It had been too long. Too much had happened. And yet my soul yearned for his, two magnets attracted together.

No. I was just angry, furious at the idea that he thought he could protect me from an imploding world. When nobody had been around to protect Olivia. Nothing more.

"How did you think you were going to protect me? Lock me up in an ivory tower, watching me grow older by the day? But at least I'd be *safe*, right? At least I'd be *protected*." I scoffed, watching his own rage roll over his face.

"Don't kid yourself, Ray. I might not have much, but at least I'm free."

"You're so bloody stubborn, you're not even hearing what you're saying." The gray of his eyes grew darker, tendons popping along his forearms where his hoodie sleeves were pushed up. "Are you really free, babydoll? Because from where I'm standing, it looks like you're still in the lair of the Kingsnakes, and I own you for the next month. Does that taste like freedom to you?"

Every drop of blood rushed to my face, setting my skin aflame. I wasn't a possession, a trophy to be set on the wall. I was my own person. Freedom came in more than one form. "No one owns me, Ray. Least of all you."

"Oh, you don't have to worry about me," he snapped. "I figured that out a long time ago when I gave a girl my heart, only for her to crush it into a million pieces."

A knife of pain pierced my chest when I realized what he must have felt when I ran. But it was a new world, and I had only done what needed to be done. I shook my head, ignoring the trembling in my fingers. "We were kids. Did you really think I was going to stay based on a fantasy you were constructing for us?"

Ray gripped my shoulders once more, his voice a deadly whisper. "It wasn't a fucking fantasy for me, Mila. I told you I would protect you with my life, and I meant every word I said."

For a moment, I was stunned into silence. Had he really been harboring these feelings for this long? Even though I ran away, leaving him and everything I had ever known behind?

"Ray, I..."

"Just shut up, Mila. Shut up for two goddamn seconds. I have so much to tell you. And yet, none of it matters, does it?" He sighed, a sound that weighed more than the world. His gray eyes pierced mine. He slid his hands up my neck, along my cheeks, so close his breath brushed against my lips. I forced my body to not react, not cave to the touch I had dreamed about for so long. "None of it fucking matters anymore."

Before I could turn away, he pressed his lips to mine, kissing me in a way that made all the time apart insignificant.

His mouth on mine erased all the years between us, and I couldn't help the moan that slipped out. Ray's mouth curled up in a smile where his was still pressed to mine.

His hand slipped under my shirt. *God.* I hadn't been touched in so long, would I even remember what to do? Would my body? And all the while, Ray had been here, working for the Kingsnakes, and...

I pushed away from him, and confusion ran across his face. "I thought you said you don't breed the girls here."

Ray's face relaxed, his expression shifting to a small smile. "This isn't breeding, and you aren't one of the girls." He removed his hand from under my shirt, toying with a strand of hair resting against my neck. Even the smallest touch from him sent me into a desperate tailspin, and I wasn't sure how I had managed so long without him.

Why had I run away in the first place?

But still I narrowed my gaze, ignoring my body's reaction to his touch.

53

"If this isn't breeding, what is it then? *Making love?* Because I sure as hell don't do that. We used to, but that was then, in a different world. Not this one."

The hand toying with my hair slid to my scalp, tangling in the strands and pulling my head back to look up at him. The sweet, gentle boy I had known in university was long gone, replaced by this man who knew how to get what he wanted. "This is fucking, Mila. And you want it as badly as I do."

God, I did. But wouldn't it be weak to cave to his touch, especially in the den of wrongdoings I found myself in? I wasn't sure I cared, even though I knew I should. It had just been so damn long. Too long. One stolen moment couldn't hurt, surely. And it wasn't like it would affect anyone else's situation around me. One slip of control, and then I could be all business. Except...

"What about Ella?" Ray's brows furrowed, his hand tightening in my hair. Damn, it felt good.

"Ella?"

I tried to nod, but couldn't under Ray's firm grip. "You said you're here for Avery and Ella. I'm assuming Ella must be your wife, or girlfriend, or something. And I'm going to guess she doesn't know about the Kingsnakes, or me."

Please say you don't care.

He let out a low chuckle, the sound bringing me back to a different place, a better time. "Ella is my youngest sister. You don't know about her because she was born after you left."

"Oh." I felt foolish, certain a blush would quickly spread across my cheeks. But damn, I was relieved. "Okay."

"Do you think you can keep any other questions to yourself until after I've dealt with a decade's worth of needing you?" Ray dove his face further into my neck, pressing hard kisses against my tender skin.

His touch overwhelmed me, darkening my senses until there was no more motel. No more Kingsnakes. No more Collapse, or years spent apart. Everything bled away, until it was just Ray's hands on my body, taking control in a way I'd forgotten how much I'd missed.

"Stop talking and fuck me," I murmured, resting my hands on his denim-clad hips and pulling them closer.

"I knew you'd see it my way." His mouth covered mine, planting desperate kisses that I eagerly returned.

I shouldn't have worried. My body responded to him as easily as it ever had. Better, if anything, probably from the years of isolation and solitude. I groaned against his lips, enjoying the way his breath grew heavier and heavier.

His hand tugged at my scalp, controlling me and moulding me to his will. His other hand slipped under my threadbare shirt, trailing a path of goosebumps as he moved higher up my waist, gliding over my breast.

For a moment I was insecure, my breath catching in my throat. Would he still find me attractive after this many years? The Collapse had eaten away at the curves of my hips and the swell of my breasts. It wasn't something I normally paid attention to – too focused on staying alive to care. But here, with Ray's hands re-discovering every inch of my body, I was suddenly aware of all the changes I had gone through since we had seen each other last.

Ray pulled lightly at my hair, commanding my eyes upwards. "Stop overthinking things, babydoll."

I smirked, shaking my head as much as I could in his tight grasp. Of course he still knew me after all these years. "I'm not."

Another heavy kiss, his tongue darting into my mouth, before a long, slow slide. My pussy throbbed, aching to be filled. "You were," he whispered as he pulled back. "But I don't mind. I'll fuck all of those thoughts out of you." His tongue dragged down my neck, exploring my collarbone in a way he knew used to drive me crazy. "Every. Last. One."

I couldn't control myself. He kissed me furiously, tugging my shirt over my head. I was trying to undo his belt buckle at the same time, refusing to let our lips part. He kicked his pants off, awkwardly tearing his hoodie over his head.

I only had a moment to notice the thick black snake tattooed across his heart before my attention was drawn elsewhere. His cock was everything I remembered – thick, long, and always ready for me. I was desperate for him to return to me.

He broke our kiss, only to put his mouth at my breast, sucking hard at my nipple. I was making sounds I'd never heard before, but I couldn't help it. Ray looked up at me with a serious expression, but laughter in his eyes.

"You're gonna have to be a bit quieter, babydoll. The girls don't normally get so into it. You'll make the other brothers jealous." The thought sobered me. All around me, in this motel of depravity, girls were in this exact situation, but against their will.

Could I really do this now? Ray smoothed my hair away from my face. "Don't let the thoughts get to you. They'll destroy you. We're all just doing what we have to do to survive. And right now, we both need this to make it through another day."

I shook away the dark feelings and the looming thoughts. Survival mode had gotten me this far, and it would see me through the rest. "Make them go away," I murmured. In Ray's eyes, I saw everything he had been through, everything he had suffered since the Collapse. And somewhere in the midst of all that destruction, I could see the tiniest glimmer of light.

He nodded, and pressed his body harder into mine. And even harder, his hands tightening around my hair and body. Urgency leached through his touch, making my heart race and my pussy tighten with anticipation. The backs of my knees hit the edge of the mattress, and I reclined back. Ray landed on top of me, propping himself up on his forearms. "Pants off," he demanded.

I cocked my head. The finality to his tone did something to my body I wasn't sure I wanted to acknowledge, but I also didn't want Ray thinking he had all the power in our current situation.

His eyes lit up. "I own you for the next month, Mila. Might as well get used to it now, because I plan on taking full advantage of having you all to myself."

I wanted to fight, to protest. But I also wanted Ray inside me. So I reached between us, pulling my pants down the best I could, until Ray had to sit up and help me the rest of the way.

Now there was nothing between us. No clothes or protection, masks or distances. He ran his eyes over my body, taking in every bit of skin, and every scar. "Fuck, babydoll. I swear you're the only person who could come out of the apocalypse hotter than before."

I smiled and shook my head, pulling him by his shoulders to lie over me again. He held himself up on one arm, using his other hand to slide down my waist, over my thighs, and between my legs. I cursed under my breath as he found the wet heat waiting for him, dragging his finger through my desire and need.

Our eyes met as he slipped one finger inside my aching pussy, and then another. He knew. He knew exactly what his presence did to me, and the way my release coiled deep inside, spiraling thanks to his curving, pulsing fingers.

I moaned, my free hand tugging at the thin bed sheets underneath me. Ray drove me to the brink of insanity, fucking me with his fingers before he eventually pulled away, leaving me alone and empty. Before I could sit up and protest I felt the thick head of his cock pressing against me.

We both cried out – softly, so as to keep the secret – as Ray drove his cock inside, fitting to me the same he always had. We lay like that for a moment, connected, staring at each other in wonder. It was just for a split second, before Ray moved his hips. He drove himself deeper with each stroke, as if trying to hammer a reminder that he had been here before. And now once again we were together after all of these years. My release snuck up on me quicker than I could stop it, and my eyes began to close.

A hand at my neck startled me into staring into Ray's gaze once more. His hand tightened around my throat, demanding my full attention. "You're not coming unless you come with me."

I nodded, unable to take my eyes off this man I once knew so well. I arched my neck into his grasp, daring him to take more. He groaned, his body moving faster as we both climbed higher and higher. His hand tightened with each stroke. His hips ground against mine, and if he didn't come soon I was going to break whether he liked it or not. Thankfully he released my neck, slamming his hand down on the bed next to my head. "Now, Mila. Come *now*."

I let go of all the tension, my body caving to its orgasm. He was still pumping, a less rhythmic motion now, whispering my name as he collapsed on top of me.

Eventually Ray rolled off, pulling down the blankets, and encouraging me to crawl underneath them. He curled up behind me, covering my back as if to protect me.

He tucked the worn comforter around my shoulders, stroking my hair. "Sleep. You need the rest."

I nodded, burrowing deeper into the covers. It wasn't my tent, and I was nowhere near safe, but sleep was essential to stay alive. I needed to restore my strength. "Will you stay?" The words slipped out before I could consider how weak they made me seem. *Shit.*

Ray groaned. "Believe me, I wish I could. But it's not safe for either of us. Besides, I need to get home to the girls."

The girls. His whole reason for being here, his sisters. I should've known he would never be here for the power.

"Tomorrow, if you have a chance, find Hannah. She's a friend of mine from high school. She'll show you the ropes and keep you safe. I'll be back as soon as I can." I rested my head back against the solidity of his chest and the steady beat of his heart.

"Hannah," I murmured, half asleep. *Hannah.* I wanted to ask him something, but the thought was pulled away, lulled by the promise of sleep.

Before I drifted off, I could've sworn I heard him whispering softly into my ears. "Maybe there can be more than survival."

SIX

Ray

I was already imagining excuses I could use to see Mila again tomorrow. Brothers were only supposed to show up every other night for breeding, so it would look suspicious if I showed up again the day after, but I needed to see her again for my own sanity.

I just needed to figure out what kind of excuse Luke or any of the other brothers would buy. Really, I needed more than an excuse. I needed to buy time.

Because I had made up my mind, and no matter what else this world or the Kingsnakes threw my way, my decision was made. I was going to get my sisters and Mila out of the city, to safety. To freedom. To the rest of our lives.

If I didn't bear Mila's scratch marks on my chest and back, I could've convinced myself it was a dream. All of it. Her presence in the motel, the night we had just spent together.

All of it could've been chalked up to some kind of sick fever dream, designed to torment and drive me crazy.

I stuffed my hands into my jean pockets as I walked the streets toward my apartment. Mila was sleeping soundly when I left. I didn't want to leave her, especially not in the hands of a bunch of degenerates.

But I also knew, in a twisted sort of way, that she was relatively safe there.

The majority of the brothers kept to the code and wouldn't lay a hand on another brother's girl. Dogberry was another matter, but he had also left the motel before I had, so she would be safe from him for the day.

Thankfully my building had been built in the era of exterior fire escapes. We were able to use it to enter the window of our second floor "suite." All suite meant was we had a bedroom separate from the kitchen, and a bathroom we didn't have to share with our neighbors.

It was a luxury, really, especially in a time when the indoor stairwell was unusable because it had been transformed into another apartment. This building had been my university apartment before the Collapse, and I had stubbornly managed to hang onto it thanks to my job at the mill.

I wouldn't – couldn't – subject the girls to other living conditions out on the streets of this new world.

Our suite cost me most of my Kingsnake cut, and my soul, but at least we had a locking door.

Water, most days. The girls were safe, for the most part.

I knocked on the door, my heart tightening with the late hour, but I knew Avery would be awake.

She always was until I got home. And then she collapsed in bed next to her younger sister, curling around her protectively the same way I did to Mila tonight.

Sure enough, a sliver of Avery's face peeked out between the faded curtains, before she unlocked and unlatched the door. She yawned as she let me in, pushing her tangle of blonde curls away from her face in a motion I found all too familiar. "You're late tonight," she muttered.

"I know. I'm sorry." I pulled my sleeves lower over my wrists, as if that could hide my nightly transgressions. I stepped over the threshold and fastened the series of locks. "I got caught up at work." *Caught up with Mila.*

I turned around to see Avery looking at me with crossed arms, every inch the scolding mother instead of the preteen sister she should've been. My heart ached for the childhood she was missing. "I know what you do at night, Ray. I'm not a baby like Ella. I know where you go."

Well, shit. I collapsed onto the sofa, the springs complaining from my weight. "Don't call your sister a baby. You know she hates it." I was exhausted, and this was not a conversation I wanted to have with my younger sister, regardless of my mental state.

Avery scoffed before sitting next to me. I turned to look at her, a miniature replica of our mother. I had been a teenage pregnancy, my father long gone before the Collapse was even a bad rumor. Avery and Ella's father had left too, but not until after the Collapse. He had been the only dad I'd ever known. He'd felt responsible for all of us.

Responsible enough that one day, when food got short, he shouldered up a backpack and kissed us all goodbye.

There was word of work in the next state over, and the payment would keep us all fed for months. But he never returned, and we never found out what happened to him.

Ella took after him, all dark hair and long limbs. But Avery and I looked like our mother. We both had the personality too – stubborn, sometimes too brash for our own good.

"Ella isn't awake. And are you really going to pretend like I didn't just call you out?"

"Jesus, Avery. Do we need to have this talk now?"

She narrowed her gray eyes at me, so like my own. "Yes. Because if Ella is awake, you'll just use her as an excuse. I think I deserve to know the truth about where you go every night."

I closed my eyes, beating my head against the back of the couch. I wanted to shower. I wanted to sleep. I wanted to go back in time, before the Collapse, and take my family somewhere safe. I hoped the beaches were still a respite from the real world, a hidden sanctuary. It was a fool's dream. Even the beaches wouldn't be safer. "If you already know where I go, why are you asking?"

"Because I want to hear you say it," she whispered. Whispering was unlike Avery, and I opened my eyes to stare at her once more. She sat still, a question written all over her face. "Mrs. Mullins from downstairs said you stole her granddaughter from her bed when she was sleeping. I told her she was a liar." Mrs. Mullins was the neighbor directly beneath us.

She was a gossip, and I wished I could keep her and her big mouth away from my sisters.

But Avery still shouldn't provoke her. Gossips were dangerous people in the city. One wrong word to the wrong person... "You shouldn't aggravate her. She's nothing but a bored old woman."

"So you're not a Kingsnake who steals unsuspecting girls from their beds?" Avery cocked her head, giving me an out. But she wanted honesty. I had to give it to her.

I sighed. "I'm a Kingsnake. The mill let me go, and we were going to lose the apartment. I couldn't let that happen. I did what I had to do – for all of us."

She nodded, absorbing the new information with a blank look on her face. It was a similar expression to the one Mila had worn, on her knees in front of the Kingsnakes. "And Mrs. Mullins' granddaughter?"

I sat up straight, looking dead into Avery's eyes. "I do *not* kidnap women. I do the bare minimum of what the Kingsnakes require of me, and only to keep you and Ella safe. But I promise you, Avery. I have never stolen a woman."

Avery smiled sadly. "Do you really think you'll be able to keep us safe our entire lives? There's going to come a day when you aren't here to protect us."

My heart tightened, her words a reflection of what Mila had said to me at the motel. Maybe I was crazy, thinking I could protect those I loved. But to me, it was crazier not to try. I had to do what I could, no matter the consequences. "I'm going to do my best."

Avery opened her mouth, ready to say something, and then closed it quickly. She shook her head. "I'm gonna go to bed. I'll see you in the morning."

With quiet footsteps, she left the room. I dragged my hands over my face. Maybe all of this was some messed up fantasy I believed in.

Thinking I could keep my sisters safe, get us all away from the city, and the Kingsnakes. Imagining what freedom – real freedom – would taste like. But I couldn't give up hope.

Not even as I sold my soul, night after night, woman after woman. I just hoped I had enough left of me to enjoy it once I got there. I got to my feet and walked to the small bathroom.

The girls' bedroom was on the way, and I poked my head in to find Avery already asleep, and soft snores coming from Ella. Their connection made me smile, and broke my heart at the same time. I would protect them, whatever the cost.

I hadn't showered at the motel, trying to make the most of every minute I had with Mila. I desperately needed to shower now. It hadn't been a typical night, to be sure, but I still needed to wash off the smells of the motel, and the lingering feelings that stuck around after any time spent with my "brothers."

Before I stepped into the bathroom, I paused in the small hallway. I was silent, making sure my sisters were actually asleep before I dropped to my knees and shifted the loose floorboard. Under it, covered by the old replica Persian carpet, was a decent-sized hole. Here, I kept my stash. I hadn't even told Avery about my hiding place, needing to keep the danger, and the hope, to myself.

In here, I stored non-perishables I got from the Kingsnakes, ready-to-eat military meals that would keep for years. There were a few thin blankets, excess water, and even a small bit of cash I had managed to scrounge together. Everything was stuffed into a couple backpacks, in case of emergency. Or, as my heart demanded, in case of a chance to escape.

Tonight, I added a flashlight and extra batteries to the backpacks, stolen from the motel's common room when no one was looking. As I zippered it back up, I did a quick visual inventory of my supplies. They were meager, but enough to get us started. Would it be enough for myself, my sisters, *and* Mila though?

I shook my head, closing the floor back up and replacing the carpet. What was I thinking, including Mila in my hopeless escape plan when I had only seen her for the first time in years tonight?

Because you'd never leave her behind, my brain whispered. No. I wouldn't. Never again. Even if the first time, *she* had left *me* behind. I stood, brushing off my knees and stepped into the bathroom to start the shower.

No hot water tonight, but at least there was water. Small miracles, right? I took the small sliver of homemade soap off the ledge, scrubbing myself thoroughly. I didn't want to wash off the traces of Mila, the reminders that she was here, she was *back*, but I knew I wouldn't be able to sleep unless I rid myself of any residue of being associated with the Snakes at all. I stood under the cool water, letting it run over my body as I thought back to the motel.

Mila was thinner than when I had seen her last, her youthful curves replaced by the muscles and strength necessary to survive in this life.

The weak didn't last long. But God, the way her body responded to mine, how wet she was by my touch alone... she would always be the most beautiful woman in the world to me.

Fucking hell. The cold water did nothing to diminish my desire for Mila, and I shivered as I remembered the way she had breathed my name when I pressed my hand against her delicate throat. She wasn't the same woman, but neither was I the same man.

Somehow, I didn't think she minded. Our bodies still fit together, all of our jagged edges locking into place. First, I wouldn't have been able to sleep thinking about the motel. Now, even clean, I knew I wouldn't be able to sleep without dealing with the growing hard-on between my legs.

I gripped my cock in my fist, propping myself up against the slick shower wall with my free hand. I could imagine Mila on her knees in front of me. Not because she had to be, but because she wanted to be. Smiling up at me with a grin that always seemed to make my heart stop beating – the one everyone else saw as innocent, but only I knew hid the dirty thoughts racing through her mind. Her hand would circle my cock, pumping slowly at first, and I would groan and let her take control. She would pick up speed, licking her deliciously full bottom lip as she focused.

Shit. Her sexy smile would always be the death of me.

I moaned softly, my need pulling me from my daydream and back into my yellowed shower. I was a goner as I edged myself toward orgasm, the memory of Mila's dangerous eyes pushing me closer. My orgasm was building, and I whispered her name as I came, my release splashing against the faded tiles.

I shook the water out of my hair, my heartbeat settling back to normal.

Fucking Mila.

I had gone years without her, and now I couldn't function for an hour away from her. I snapped the water off and grabbed one of the once-white towels from its hook.

My footsteps were silent as I walked down the hall, stepping over the floorboards I knew creaked to avoid waking up the girls. For months, my sex drive had been shot to hell. The Collapse, everything that happened with the Kingsnakes, and just plain survival, had zapped me of any and all energy. Mila returned, and suddenly I was a desperate teenager again.

Ridiculous. I grabbed an old pair of sweatpants from my small pile of clothes, and found my blanket next to the tv. My bed had been the couch since my mom and the girls had moved in, and I made myself as comfortable as I could.

SEVEN

Mila

I woke up to an empty bed and a couple of girls screaming down the hall. Something about a stolen boyfriend, or some other garbage I didn't care to get involved with. I rolled over, curling my pillow over my head so I didn't have to hear.

Living in a dorm was the worst, especially when said dorm mates couldn't keep their hands to themselves. My alarm set to wake me up for my first class would be going off soon, and I wanted to sleep every minute I could before Olivia barged into my room.

How anyone could be as much of a morning person as her, I had no idea. The pillow did nothing to muffle the sounds of the fight, and as I slowly woke up, I realized where I was.

This wasn't university. I wasn't in my dorm, waiting for my alarm clock to go off.

In fact, when was the last time I had even set an alarm?

I was in a motel, in the hands of the Kingsnakes, and girls I didn't know were fighting for reasons I definitely didn't want to know about.

I flopped over, the hard springs of the mattress digging into my hips and back. Not the most comfortable bed in the world, but after sleeping in the woods for years I wasn't about to complain.

The indentation of Ray's lean body was still cut into the thin mattress next to me. *Ray.* When I had fled the city, I swore to leave it all behind. Memories only rubbed salt into wounds I would rather forget.

So I had decided to forget it all – easier said than done, of course. Olivia's disappearance, school, my future, *Ray.* Yet the second he pulled down his mask and I looked at his sculpted face and into those gray eyes that always seemed to see right through me, I knew. There had never been a chance for me to forget any of it. My body remembered the way he touched me, the way he made me come alive in his hands.

But I also knew I couldn't stay here. It would be dangerous to leave, but I'd rather die trying than be cycled around every month, passed from brother to brother. I lucked out with Ray this month, but I had no idea how much sway he held within the Kingsnakes, and couldn't tell what next month would bring. Meaning, I had approximately 29 days to get my ass out of here.

Would he come with me? The thought sprang to my mind unbidden. Could he leave everything behind and follow me into the unknown?

It wasn't like there was much to leave behind anymore, aside from a solid roof over one's head. Otherwise, it was mostly safer outside the city limits.

We'd have to bring Avery, of course, and Ella too. I didn't know how old she was, which could be problematic. If she was too young, Ray wouldn't risk bringing her, but he also wouldn't leave her behind.

And what about all the other girls, hiding behind the worn and broken motel doors? Could I really leave them behind, knowing exactly what fate I was abandoning them to?

You don't owe them anything. True, I didn't. But that didn't lessen the guilt. Not for the first time, I wished I could've been one of those people who lost their morals along with the rest of their lives.

I groaned and stretched, finding the clothes Ray had roughly discarded the night before. I yanked on my pants, remembering to check the pocket for what I had left there.

I pulled out my almost-empty lighter. The worn Florida emblem, nearly down to the bare aluminum, still brought a smile to my face. This would definitely come in handy, so long as I could keep it hidden.

I didn't want to leave the relative safety of my room, but the screaming was getting louder, and my stomach was growling. The girls, while thin, didn't seem to be starving, so I had to assume there was food for us *somewhere* in this decrepit establishment. I tugged on my sneakers and cracked open the door.

Down the hall, a tall brunette was pulling the hair of a blonde girl.

"You *knew* he was going to choose me this month! I fucking *told you* he was choosing me! But you just *had* to waltz in here with those ghastly tits sticking out of that nasty-ass dress, and lure him away from me!"

The blonde sneered, trying to claw at the brunette's face but missing by an inch or two. "It's not *my* problem Brother Hamlet is obsessed with me. Maybe if you had more to offer than a flat fucking ass, he would've picked you."

Lord, I did not want to get involved with this. Did these girls not realize what they were fighting over? Which guy they wanted to breed them, to keep them here against their will?

And then it hit me, as the brunette gasped and whirled back to slap the blonde. The same way I took control over my life by escaping to the woods, these girls were asserting what little control they had over their lives. Picking out which guy they wanted to choose them, acting like they had a say in the matter. It probably made the horrific situation more liveable.

I looked around the hallway as the verbal fight dissolved into physical blows. A small group of girls gathered around the fight – probably the most excitement they'd had in weeks. But other girls peeked out of their doors, like me. Across the hall, a tiny redhead offered me a delicate smile. I smiled back, unsure.

Did I want to make friends here, or did I just want to get the hell out before the guilt set in? The redhead looked both ways, then tiptoed across the hall to my room. She pushed past me, but left the door open a crack.

"They don't like us being in the same room alone with the door shut. But apparently hallway fist fights are okay." She rolled her eyes and flashed me a friendly smile. I immediately liked her. "I'm Hannah."

Hannah. "Ra... uh, Brother Prospero told me to find you. I'm Mila." Hannah was small and pale, too doll-like for my mind to make sense of in the dirty motel. Out in the hall, one of the girls shrieked, and someone clapped.

Hannah's smile widened. "You don't need to worry about the formalities with me. Ray and I knew each other in high school. The Collapse made a small world smaller, I guess." She shrugged and tipped her head to one side. "He spoke about you once, you know. I don't think he meant to. You must really mean a lot to him."

My mind immediately wondered why Ray would've said my name. He said he didn't breed the girls, but he had fucked me last night. And he knew Hannah. Would he have had sex with her, pulling her red hair away from her face so he could watch her fall apart? Did he whisper my name as he came inside her? The idea made me squeamish in a way I couldn't describe. I didn't have a claim over him. Ray was his own person, free to live his life however he wanted to.

Tell that to the tiny ache in the bottom of my heart...

The petite redhead interrupted my thoughts. "Just so you know, Ray and I, we never... uh... it's not like that." A bright red blush spread up her neck and across her cheeks.

I tried to pretend like that hadn't been exactly what I was envisioning. "Ray and I haven't been together for a very long time." Even though it was the truth, it tasted like a lie.

74

We hadn't been together. But last night also felt like no time had passed.

"Still, I'll let you know. Ray's not like that." She shrugged, and stepped toward the door. "Come on. I'll show you where to find the cereal that isn't stale before everyone gets bored of the fight." With no other option than to trust her, I followed her out the door and into the hallway Ray had led me down the night before.

It was different in the day, sunlight streaming in through the partially boarded-up windows. It made the corners less spooky, the edges less jagged. But it also illuminated the wear on the wood, souvenirs of everything that happened over the last decade.

Hannah made her way down the stairs, toward the common room where the Choosing had taken place. As we walked, she spoke to me quietly over her shoulder. "On days we don't have Ceremonies or a Choosing, we're left to our own devices for the most part. The doors are locked with keys, obviously, and they leave a couple of the lower-ranking brothers to keep watch over us. But the day is mostly ours. Sometimes we even have water and can alternate showers."

A shower. With running water. I knew the water wouldn't be hot – gas was long gone, and electricity was iffy at best.

But I couldn't remember the last time I had bathed inside and not out in the open. Still, a thought nagged at me. "Why don't you just leave? Surely it wouldn't be that hard to overpower a couple guys. Hannah shrugged. "They leave the brothers on duty with guns. It may not be the life I envisioned for myself, but it's better than being dead most days."

She paused, chewing on her lip. "Some of the girls... they *like* being here." Even horrified, I could understand how being a captive could be tempting to some of these girls. Sure enough, just like Hannah had said, one of the brothers sat next to the door, watching us as we walked to the other side of the room.

"Good morning, Brother Tybalt," Hannah murmured as we passed. The Kingsnake tipped his head toward us in acknowledgement, but said nothing. We stepped through the door into an ancient kitchen. "How can you tell them apart?" I whispered, not knowing what was allowed and what wasn't in this surreal environment.

Hannah hummed, opening a cupboard with only one door remaining. She stuck half her body inside to rummage through the mess. "You learn pretty quickly based on their voices, and how they act. Tybalt isn't usually a bad one, as long as you don't piss him off. Others you'll want to steer clear of completely." I wanted to ask her more, to know which brothers I needed to avoid, but she was already pulling out a plastic bag of what looked like kids' cereal.

"Here we go! One of the brothers raided a storage facility a few weeks ago and found loads of unopened cereal. I've hidden some of it at the very back, but I'll share it with you." I smiled, oddly charmed at the easy comradery we had developed.

I wasn't surprised Ray hung around with Hannah, but I was shocked at how long she had managed to survive after the Collapse. In my personal experience, most of the sweet ones were long gone.

I took the proffered bowl filled with the neon hoops, and sat cross legged on the dusty floor. Hannah sat across from me with her own bowl. The cereal was dry, of course. Even the Kingsnakes wouldn't be able to procure milk that didn't exist. "How long have you been here?"

She chewed slowly, savoring her meal – a look I knew all too well. "The city, or *here*?"

"Here." I took a handful of my own cereal. Slightly chewy, but Hannah was right – it wasn't overly stale. "When did they... take you?"

"About a year ago?" Hannah was quiet, staring into space past me. She sighed. "Yeah, I think it must be almost a year at this point. I haven't gotten pregnant, so if it was longer than that I'd know. The ones that don't get pregnant apparently don't stick around for longer."

My heart froze in my chest. "Where do they go?"

She shrugged, casually, as if she wasn't discussing her own potential near future. "Who knows? One day they're here, the next day they're gone. Anything's got to be better than this bullshit though."

I was about to say something in retort, something hopeful, uplifting, but really, what was there to say? What were the chances I'd be able to get myself out of here in a month, let alone myself *and* Hannah? It didn't matter though, because loud footsteps clattered through the doorway, interrupting our quiet breakfast.

"Well, if it isn't Little Orphan Annie and the new girl who thinks she can steal another girl's man." My jaw tightened, already annoyed without caring to see who stood behind me.

Hannah looked up past me, and then back at me with a shake of her head. "It's not worth it, Mila."

I turned around to see the girl who had been in line next to me last night. Lauren? No. Laura. She wore the same dress, same shoes, and an expression that screamed trouble. "Good morning to you, too," I said, taking another bite of my dry cereal.

"It would've been a good morning, if you hadn't stolen my man on the first night here," she accused, slapping her hands on her hips. I did everything in my power to not roll my eyes. As far as I was aware, we were captives in the middle of an apocalypse, not in a high school cafeteria.

"Look, if you're wanting to fight, I think two girls upstairs already beat you to it. I just showed up here yesterday and did what they told me to do." I raised an eyebrow at her. "You realize I had no say in who chose me, right?"

Laura sneered. "Brother Prospero was supposed to choose me yesterday, and he would've if you hadn't shown up. You could've said no when they offered him to you."

I set my bowl of cereal down, staring up at her in disbelief. Surely, she couldn't be serious. "Are you kidding me right now? How was I supposed to know any of this?"

"Maybe if you'd spent a little less time sucking dick when you got here, and a little more time learning your place, you'd know we have a hierarchy amongst the girls. And new girls are on the bottom of the totem pole." She smirked, a cruel twist of her lips. "Brother Dogberry is probably more your speed anyways, *bitch*."

"Laura," Hannah hissed. "Stop it."

I considered de-escalating the situation, explaining to Laura that Brother Brutus was the one who made the decision. But it was too late, because Laura was already circling, and my fight instincts kicked in. "Excuse me?"

Laura's grin grew wider, a shark smelling blood in the water. "You heard me. The only way a new girl would've landed Brother Prospero is on her knees begging for Kingsnake dick."

I was fuming. I was angry for myself, for Hannah behind me, and for life throwing this in my face. For Ray, who had to put up with this bullshit, and for the girls getting trapped in here with sleazy men and sharp-tongued women.

How was any of this fair? Hannah was saying something behind me, but I couldn't hear her through my fury. Years of suppressed rage, brewing to a boil, now focused on this blonde snake in front of me. She may not be a Kingsnake, but she was a serpent just the same.

I pushed against her shoulders, shoving her backwards. "Who the hell do you think you are, talking to me like that?"

Laura stumbled, but quickly regained her balance. "Your superior, bitch. And you might as well get used to it, because you're going to be under my thumb for a long time. The first thing you're going to do is go to Brother Brutus and tell him a mistake has been made, and that we're switching brothers."

I took a step closer. "And if I don't?"

She smiled, her yellowed teeth at odds with the rest of her carefully curated self. "Honey, I'll make your life a living hell."

I smiled back. "Good thing it already is."

I turned to the side, eyeing the other girls watching carefully, and giving Laura a chance to step closer. Once I heard her clattering footsteps, I swung my leg behind her, catching her off guard on her too-tall heels, and she tumbled to the floor with a loud thump of her ass.

Laura glared. "You fucking bitch!" she screeched. "You'll be sorry for this."

"Just try me, Barbie. Fucking try me. You'll be dead before you lay a finger on me." Hannah was pulling me backwards, telling me to be quiet, but it was too late. We had already drawn a crowd, everyone eager to see who the new girl was fighting with.

Unfortunately, included in that crowd was Brother Tybalt. "What the hell is going on here?" he thundered, scowling at all of us through his heavy bone mask. "It's not even noon, and I'm having to clean up a fight?"

Laura looked up at me with a knowing glance, and immediately turned to Tybalt with tears in her eyes. "It was all the new girl, Brother Tybalt! I came down for breakfast, and she just got all feral and crazy and told me she was going to kill me!"

God, I had forgotten how well some girls could play the game. "That's not even remotely true." But even as the words left my mouth, I knew it didn't matter. I was standing, Hannah pulling me back, as Laura lay sprawled on the floor. I knew how it looked.

Brother Tybalt glared at me. "It's your first day, and you can't even keep it together? Isolation time for you. Maybe you'll learn to behave on day two."

He reached for my arm, wrapping a tight hand around my bicep. I immediately pushed him away.

"Don't fucking touch me," I snapped. The girls had backed up, giving us a wide berth. At my words, they gasped.

"Excuse me?" Brother Tybalt's voice was eerily calm. "Did you just speak back to a Kingsnake?"

I wasn't sure what the rules were here – Hannah and I obviously hadn't gotten that far – but I was pretty sure I had just broken a big one. It was too late to do anything but double down now. "And if I did?"

The anger in Tybalt's gaze simmered into something else, something I regretted immediately. He grabbed my arm again, pulling me through the crowd of girls as I dragged my feet, attempting to slow him down.

"I'll teach you a lesson in respect, that's what. Brutus will have my head, but it'll be worth it to enlighten the new girl in how we do things around here."

"You're not going to touch me," I hissed, trying to pull away before he could reach the stairs.

Tybalt turned around, ready to snap something at me, but his eyes widened. I could only imagine what he saw behind me, but I hoped like hell it was enough to save my ass.

"Brother Tybalt, what the hell are you doing with my female?" Ray snarled.

Saved was one word for it.

EIGHT

Ray

I should've known not to leave Mila alone for more than five minutes, let alone the better part of a morning. What was I expecting, leaving her in a cesspool of heightened emotions and corruption? And of course it had to be Brady – Brother Tybalt – who was on duty this morning.

I should've checked before I left last night. I should've done a lot of things, honestly.

But I had so many things on my mind. My weak excuse of leaving a hoodie behind had worked with the brother when I knocked on the front door. For now. I didn't have a lot of sway with the Kingsnakes based on my tenure alone, but most of them knew my relationship with Luke. They knew to stay out of my way. But arriving to find Brady dragging a fuming Mila up the stairs was certainly not the best start to my day.

What the hell was Mila thinking? I told her to keep her head down, and to find Hannah. "I asked you a question, *brother*." My voice left no room for argument. He knew I had caught him red-handed.

Luke didn't like to see the brothers using the women who weren't theirs for the month, or outside their Ceremony rights. Morals, you know. Brady had a temper, but he'd never use it on me for fear of repercussions.

Brady immediately dropped Mila's arm, opening and closing his mouth like a fish gasping for air. "The new... the new girl... she..."

"Spit it out. I don't have all day." I snapped my eyes toward Mila, giving her a warning glance to stay quiet while I dealt with this. She stepped sideways down a stair, closer to me and further away from Brady.

"The new girl started a fight in the kitchen. When I confronted her, she disrespected me. In front of all the other girls. I was just taking her to isolation. Nothing else." He had stopped stuttering, but I could see the blatant lie in his eyes.

"Just to isolation? No other means of teaching *my* female respect?" I forced myself to maintain my composure, even as my stomach churned with the idea of *Brady* laying a hand on Mila.

"Well... uh..." Brady wouldn't meet my gaze, refusing to reply to my question. It didn't matter. I had my answer.

I shook my head, grabbing Mila by the wrist.

Brady would see it as a show of dominance, while really, my intentions were to keep her close.

Out of his reach.

83

"You know the rules, Brother Tybalt. I'm disappointed in you. Now, I'm going to take my female to her room, and we're going to forget this entire mess. Go clean up the shitshow in the kitchen before Brother Brutus finds out."

"Yes, brother." Like a good little sheep, at the mention of his leader he pushed past us, disappearing around the corner.

I watched him go, then turned to go back up the stairs, pulling Mila along behind me.

"Ray," Mila whispered.

"It's Brother Prospero," I ground out. "And don't talk."

"But Ra- Brother Prospero. I want to explain."

I pulled on her wrist harder, not turning around. My anger was still fuming beneath my skin, itching uncomfortably. I didn't want to take it out on Mila, but it needed a release. And the hallway wasn't a safe place for it.

"Don't. Talk." I knew Mila well enough to know she wouldn't give up. As soon as we got to the top of the stairs, I turned left instead of right, which would have led us toward her room. I threw open the door at the end of the hall, and closed it behind us.

I knew we were in a small room lined with shelves, once a linen closet. Mila wouldn't know where we were, because darkness surrounded us like a shroud.

The only visible light was the sunlight seeping in from the crack under the door. Slowly, my eyes adjusted to the dark.

I couldn't make out Mila's delicate features, or the expression on her face, but I could see enough to know where she was.

84

Finally, I addressed her. "What the *hell* were you thinking?" I snapped, keeping my voice low.

Brady would be the only Kingsnake here until dark, but I wasn't about to take any chances. "I fucking told you to keep to yourself. Instead you pick a *fight* with one of the brothers? Are you *trying* to get yourself killed?"

Mila huffed, and I wouldn't have been surprised if she had stomped her foot to go along with it. "Really, *Brother Prospero*? Who the *fuck* do you think you are? Up until yesterday, we were practically strangers. Still are, if you really think about it. We're not the same people we were back then, and we're definitely not together. You can't tell me what to do and expect me to go along with it."

"Do you think I just stopped caring about you when you left? Do you think love is something you can just turn off? Shit, Mila, we were supposed to get *married*." My eyes were fully adjusted to the dim light, and I could see the room – and Mila – much better now. I slammed my fist backwards, hitting a shelf of weak wood. It exploded into dust and slivers.

"It's been a long time, Ray. Long enough to move on." Mila coughed quietly, the dust from my outburst reaching her. "Besides, apparently your girlfriend Laura wants my head on a plate."

I groaned, the pieces falling into place. Of course Laura was involved in this. "Laura is *not* my girlfriend."

Mila laughed, a low, dry chuckle. We both fell quiet as footsteps echoed on the stairs, turning toward the bedrooms.

"That's not the story she told me. Rumor is, you were supposed to choose her this month."

"Laura is delusional! She's what we call a... Snake Charmer." I cringed at both the idea and the God-awful term. I was pissed at Brady for touching Mila, annoyed at Mila for starting shit, and now I was irritated with Laura as well.

There wasn't much I could do about Laura, which only fueled my fury. "There's a couple girls who actually *want* to be bred by the Kingsnakes. Snake Charmers. One of the brothers came up with the name, and it stuck. Laura is one of them. And seeing as I don't fuck the girls, Laura would *not* be a wise choice for me. But I guess you haven't been listening to a word I said."

Mila took a step toward me, her shadowy figure growing closer. "I have been listening. I just don't care. You can fuck whoever you want. It's none of my business. Just like what I do is none of yours," she hissed.

I stepped forward, invading Mila's personal space and waiting for her to back down. "What aren't you understanding here, babydoll? For the next month, you, and you alone, are my business."

"I haven't been your business since I was twenty," she muttered, shuffling back only slightly.

I closed the gap, pushing her further until I heard her back hit the wall. My hands rested on either side of her face. "You never stopped being my goddamn business." I was close enough to hear her breath catch in her throat. A wicked satisfaction spread through me as I realized that despite Mila's survival instincts, I still affected her. She *wanted* me.

Desire flicked hotly in the millimeter of space between our lips, a silent battle being waged to see who would break first. "You could be gone a thousand years, and you'd always be my fucking business. I think I remember telling you something along those lines," I whispered, pressing my mouth against her lips so she could feel my words as much as hear them.

Mila leaned into me, her hips shifting forward to grind against mine in a way I wasn't sure she was entirely conscious of. "You always were a dreamer."

"I dreamt you'd come back to me, and here you are." I wove my fingers into her hair, pinning her in place, and kissed her exactly how I had in every single one of my dreams. It didn't take much before her lips moved in time with mine, my kisses drawing soft moans out of her.

I didn't bother mentioning my dreams had never taken place in a dirty closet, anxiety about being caught heightening my senses with every stolen moment.

I hadn't pictured sitting back in a pile of what I could only assume were shredded newspapers as I pulled Mila down to straddle me. In my dreams, her return had always signified wide open spaces, freedom, and watching the sunset without watching my back.

But here, now, with Mila tearing her shirt over her head, arching her back as I tugged one of her perfect nipples into my mouth... None of those dreams were half as important as the reality in front of me.

"Shit, Ray," Mila murmured, leaning further and further into my touch.

I wrapped my arms around her back, pulling her even closer as I gently bit down. She ground her hips against me, and I groaned, desperate to be inside of her again.

The Collapse hadn't changed our passion for each other. If anything, it made it more tangible, a necessity, because we both knew how delicate life was. You could be planning your wedding one day, and the next day looking for your missing fiancée, fires blazing through close-knit apartment buildings like they were no more than paper.

Right now, I needed to feel more of her, no barriers between us. "Take off your pants," I ground out. I was already pushing her back, freeing my achingly hard cock from my jeans. It wouldn't be making love, not like we used to. It would be fucking, our bodies giving and taking in a way only they knew how.

Mila didn't respond, but the zip of her jeans told me she was obeying me without question. A compliant Mila... *damn*. It turned me on more than it should have. Part of me wanted to take her back to my apartment, tie her to the bed, and wait for her to beg. To punish her for the agony she had put me through for so long.

But then reality roared back, and all I wanted was her. I shuffled my pants off my legs, and Mila returned, her body straddling mine, her bare legs pressed against the outside of my thighs.

"Ray," she whispered, dragging her fingertips through my hair. I leaned forward, licking up her neck, making her shiver. "Yeah, babydoll?" I murmured in her ear, before biting down gently on her earlobe.

I could feel how wet she was for me, her desire making it easy for me to edge my way inside.

"Make me forget."

I didn't need to ask what she meant. Instead, I pulled her higher and sank inside of her wet heat. I cursed under my breath. Somehow I always forgot the bliss of Mila wrapped around me until I was once again buried inside her, and then all I wanted to do was savor every moment.

But instinct took over both of us, Mila grinding her body against me as I thrust up. Nothing in the world compared to this, fucking the woman who was fucking me back. I pulled her down harder, forcing myself deeper, and a soft sigh of pleasure escaped both of us. "Damn, Mila, you take me like such a good girl."

I did it again. And again. I pulled her hair at the scalp, exposed her neck to my lips and my teeth. Mila rode me harder, her breath coming in small pants. My own release was building. I just needed to drive both of us over the edge as Mila's hands gripped my shoulders.

Unfortunately, at that exact moment, the unmistakable sounds of footsteps were thundering up the stairs. I froze, and Mila grumbled. I pressed my hand over her mouth, forcing her to stay quiet. Hopefully they would walk by quickly.

But of course, we couldn't be so lucky.

Two girls stood at the top of the stairs leisurely engaging in conversation instead of returning to their rooms. And here I was in the closet, unmasked, with Mila on top of my dick. Exactly the position we couldn't afford to get caught in.

I willed them to leave, my cock demanding I thrust into her sweet pussy once more, but still they stayed.

Mila shifted on top of me, and I expected her to get off. Instead she slid herself back down my cock, rocking her hips against me. "What do you think you're doing?" I hissed, barely stifling a groan as she fucked herself slowly.

"I'm so close. I'll be quiet," she murmured, holding tighter to my shoulders as she pressed her body against mine.

"Liar." Mila was terrible at being quiet. But the temptation was too much. I gripped her hips, helping her to ride me. The girls outside continued to talk, and Mila continued to fuck herself on my cock. She pressed her forehead against mine as she moaned and trembled around me. I closed my eyes, pulling her through her release as my own orgasm shook through me. I wasn't sure how quiet either of us had been.

"Did you hear that?" one of the girls asked the other. My breathing slowed.

There was a beat of silence before her companion responded. "Uh, no. I think you're losing it from being in this motel for so long."

The first girl laughed, but it was cold. "You aren't wrong there."

Mila and I sat, still joined, her forehead still pressed to mine, as we waited for the girls to finally stop talking. The footsteps faded away, and I heaved a sigh of relief.

"We should get you back to your room."

"Too close of a call for you, Brother Prospero?"

Mila teased, but she was lifting off me, feeling around in the darkness for her clothing.

"Shut up." I got to my feet, zipping my pants back up and pulling my mask into place. I opened the door a crack, and light flooded into the small closet. Mila was fully dressed, so I peeked outside into the hall. "We're good. Come on."

I pulled her hand behind me as we tiptoed into her room. The moment her bedroom door closed behind us, she met my eyes and smirked. "I figured we wouldn't have to sneak around anymore once we were out of university."

I couldn't help the smile spreading across my face, or the laugh following it. She joined in, her smirk growing into a wide smile. This was what it had been like before with Mila. Easy. Happy. This was what was missing from my life.

I wasn't supposed to be on watch today, so I had time to sit with Mila in her bed and just talk. About where she'd been, and how she'd survived. About Ella, and my mother. About the Kingsnakes, and the forest. The only thing we didn't talk about was that day, the last day we'd spent together. The one where she never returned.

I wanted to know what made her run, but I didn't want to push, and she didn't offer. So we talked, the same way we always had. She curled into my side, whispering all the secrets that she kept locked inside. We caught up, until Mila's eyelids drifted closed, and I rested her down on the thin, yellowed pillow.

I watched Mila sleep, the same way she always had. Curled up to one side, tucking her knees into her chest, making herself as small as possible. Usually I would wrap my body behind hers, covering her weak side.

Always the protector, even when I didn't want to be.

But protecting the girls wasn't what we did here. Here, the protector became the villain. Funny how the end of the world changed everything in a heartbeat.

I stroked her dark hair away from her face, her freckled skin illuminated by the moonlight streaming in through the half-boarded-up window. "Why'd you leave, babydoll?" I whispered, knowing she was asleep and wouldn't hear me.

It didn't matter anyways. She had her reasons for why she left, and I had to trust they were more than her not wanting to marry me.

Because when we were together in the same room, the chemistry was still there. The electricity of a soul meeting its counterpart. My heart was being squeezed by a vice, and I could barely choke out the words that broke me. "Shit, Mila. Why'd you have to fucking leave?"

The only answer I got was a quiet sigh, Mila settling into a deeper slumber. I shook my head. I was foolish to think vocalizing my thoughts would bring me any closure.

Not right now at least. I pressed a kiss to her forehead, struggling to get off the shaky bed without waking her up, but Mila was out cold. I pulled the blanket up, tucking her in. Pausing in her doorway, I drank her in one more time, before heading back downstairs to deal with Brother Tybalt. *Asshole*.

Except by the time I made it downstairs and turned the corner, Tybalt wasn't alone.

Luke stood with him, and a few other Kingsnakes. He looked up, surprised to see me. "Brother Prospero. It isn't your night. What are you doing here?"

"I... uh..." My excuse had worked well with the brother on door duty, but I wasn't sure it would work as well with Luke. Somehow, he had a way of seeing right through me.

Maybe this was where I got caught, before I even had a chance to see where I stood with Mila. Maybe this was my end. My lie stood on the tip of my tongue, ready to watch my downfall.

Luke shook his head. "Who am I kidding? You probably heard the rumors before I did. You seem to have sources everywhere. Besides, we can use all the extra hands tonight. Get back upstairs and grab as many girls as you can."

"Not a problem, brother." I had no idea why I was grabbing girls, but I couldn't ask without revealing I had no idea what the rumor was.

"Fucking cops have left us alone for months. I pay my dues. I don't touch their families," Luke muttered, trailing behind me up the stairs. "I really don't need a fucking raid tonight."

A raid. The police were coming to raid the Kingsnakes. I had left my baby sisters at home, and the love of my life in a locked motel room directly in harm's way. Luke had said it best.

I really didn't need a raid tonight.

NINE

10 YEARS AGO

Mila

I woke up with chapped lips, a stale taste in my mouth, and a pounding headache. I rolled over on what I assumed was my bed, only to immediately roll off and hit the floor.

Apparently I had passed out on the couch, and upon sitting up, I immediately clocked the usual suspects. *Wine*. Two empty bottles sat on the cheap coffee table in front of me. Next to them was a half-empty bottle of home-distilled gin Olivia had somehow managed to procure. I wanted to retch at the sight. I scrubbed my hand over my face, regretting all of my life choices, and stumbled to my feet in desperate need of a shower.

Olivia and I had decided since we were now university seniors – basically functioning adults – our girls' nights would no longer include clubbing and Porn Star drinks, but wine and dinner.

Of course, with all the food and alcohol shortages, wine was a rare commodity. Most of the time we could only get the homemade stuff, either way too sweet or so bitter it made your lips pucker, but we made do. Last night we had made do with some homemade gin as well.

That explained the headache. My phone buzzed from my pants pocket, and I slid it out to see five texts from Ray. The buzzing was familiar from my restless dreams, and I realized my phone was what had woken me up. *Shit.*

It was later than I expected, and I had told him I would be over first thing to take Avery to the park. His mom and step-dad had both taken extra shifts on weekends, so Ray would watch his little sister, and I would spend time with both of them. I didn't mind. I loved Ray, and Avery was the sweetest little doll. But it was already eleven, and I had told him I would be there at nine.

"Liv?" I called. Hopefully one of us had made it to bed. I checked Ray's messages as I waited for her to respond.

I was an even bigger pile of garbage. I ran my hand through my hair, quickly typing out an apology text. Not that it mattered, because the little bars at the top of my screen dwindled to half a bar, and then nothing. I groaned, leaving my phone on the kitchen counter.

Cell signals had been unreliable for at least two months. I heard in my psych class that out in the country, cell service was already nonexistent. It was only a matter of time before it happened here too.

Hopefully this was just a blip, and by the time I finished my shower, the message would be sent.

I dragged my feet down the hall, knocking on Olivia's door as I passed. "Liv! It's eleven. I'm gonna take a shower and head over to Ray's." Still nothing. I frowned, but it wasn't entirely unusual for Olivia to be completely unconscious after a night of drinking.

There wasn't any hot water left by the time I jumped in the shower – unsurprising, given the late hour – but the cool water still helped to wake me up. And at least I didn't smell like gin anymore. I toweled off quickly, darting into my room for clothes. I pulled on a T-shirt and a light jacket, tugged on my running shoes, and debated if I should go knock on Olivia's door again or just leave her to sleep.

I knew she had a final coming up she was supposed to be studying for, but she was also her own person. If she wanted to sleep instead of study, that was up to her. I grabbed my phone off the counter, frowning at the lack of bars still glaring up at me from the tiny screen.

As I stepped out the door, I stopped, absentmindedly twisting the engagement ring on my finger – a small little thing, with both of us still in school. We planned to get married in June, after graduation. A small affair, since I only had Olivia, and he only had his mom and Avery. Small as the ring may be, it brought me more comfort than I anticipated. A reminder that Ray was there, watching over me. It was odd, but comforting. He looked out for me, and I needed to look out for Olivia.

I jogged down the hall, giving her bedroom door one last firm knock before opening it up. Half expecting to find the room empty, my heart pre-emptively sank. But instead, Olivia lay in bed, only her tousled blonde hair visible above her duvet. "Liv? I'm headed out. I'll see you later tonight, okay?"

"Mmmmmkoooommm," was her strangled response.

I smiled to myself. "I'm going to assume that means okay. Bye, Liv." Reassured, I left the apartment, firmly locking the door behind me.

A light drizzle started to fall as I walked the few blocks between home and the park, and I pulled the hood of my coat overhead. I weaved my apartment keys between my fingers – a makeshift weapon, *just in case*.

Most of the things we did now were *just in case*. Not going out after dark. Selling the car. Stocking up on an extra pack of painkillers when the grocery store had them in stock. Just in case. The food shortages had been slow at first. Slow enough that no one really complained until full shelves were empty. Then aisles. Food wasn't the only shortage either.

People whispered it was the end of times – the apocalypse. And once those rumors started, it didn't take people long to start turning on each other. I always thought it'd take longer for a human to turn back into an animal. Turns out, all it took was a grocery store without eggs.

People robbed and mugged other people in broad daylight. Others kidnapped babies, desperate for a child of their own.

Getting pregnant was no longer the commonplace accident it used to be. Girls began to disappear, and no one knew where they went, or if they would ever come back.

Olivia and I tried to not go out on our own without each other anymore. With both of us being psych majors, our classes were all the same. University classes were still held in person, even with the dwindling number of students – society's last grasp at normalcy. But walking the distance from our house to the park wasn't a big deal.

Across the street, I watched a young man use a clothes hanger to unlock a car parked on the road. A car I doubted was his. The door opened, he tossed the hanger to one side, and moments later peeled out of the parking space. I hid my face deeper in my hood, not wanting to be an accomplice to any crime. I didn't like to admit it, but the city scared me sometimes. People were desperate to maintain the same lifestyle they'd had before the shortages.

Seeing the park was a relief, and I wasn't surprised to see Ray's dirty-blond hair as he pushed Avery's small body in a swing. I jogged the last few feet, desperate to feel safe once more. But even the park wasn't the same as it used to be.

The tunnel was boarded up, an attempt to keep shady deals from happening while kids played. Graffiti covered every square inch of the play structure, now more neon than primary colors. And the lone remaining swing was zip-tied and duct-taped together. I knew this, because I had helped Ray fix it the last time it broke.

Avery saw me first, her eyes lighting up. "Meeeeeeeeela!"

I put on my biggest smile, the one I saved just for her. "Hey, sweet girl! Sorry I'm late."

"Yeah, Auntie Mila was too busy gett–"

I elbowed Ray with a glare. "Hey! Sensitive ears."

Ray opened up his arm, wrapping me in a tight embrace. "She's three. She won't remember that Auntie Mila was late to the park because she was hungover." Technically I would be Avery's sister-in-law soon, but auntie was easier for her, and I didn't care. Her sweet little way of saying my name made me smile every time.

"Ray!" I tried to push away from his squeeze, but he just held me tighter, hugging me until I laughed. "I am sorry though. My cell signal was crap this morning, so I couldn't even respond to your texts."

"I know. It's okay." He leaned away from me briefly to give Avery another push on the swing, before turning his face to the sky. I admired his strong profile, the cut of his jaw and his nose. He was so damn handsome and didn't even realize it. "Our power has been off and on since last night too. I'm hoping the generator survives at least until June. I'm not looking forward to writing my exams by candlelight."

I clapped my hands over my ears. "Don't say that! That's my worst nightmare." Brownouts were becoming more and more common, giving us barely enough power to charge our phones or run a nightlight, but candlelight was just so... 1773.

Ray laughed, smiling at Avery as she joined in. "It's only your worst nightmare because between you and Olivia, you'd burn your friggin' apartment down, babydoll."

He wasn't wrong. Especially once you threw homemade wine into the mix. "It's just a lot to take in. Surreal. One minute we're applying to universities, looking at dorms. Next thing we know... this." I knew what people were calling it. The Collapse. We had overstretched ourselves, and now society was collapsing in on itself, all in less than four years.

"I know what you mean. I wasn't expecting the whole family to cram into my apartment." Ray's mom, step-dad, and Avery had all moved into his small, one bedroom apartment after the cost of maintaining a whole house became too much. He nodded his chin toward the opposite side of the park. "We should probably get going."

I followed his gaze toward a small group of guys about our age. They were all dressed similarly, in dark sweaters and jeans, and were headed toward an elderly couple returning from the grocery store. I knew what was going to happen next, and I didn't want to see it. The worst part about people turning on each other was that there wasn't much we could do, besides stand by and let it happen. Ray and I had to think about Avery, and two against five wasn't exactly a fair fight.

So instead, you turned the other way and pretended not to see, even when the memories haunted your sleep.

"Fuck," I murmured, turning the other way. Ray was already slowing the swing, telling Avery we were going home. "I don't think I can do this anymore."

"Do what?" Ray focused on Avery, pulling her hat further down her mop of hair, but I could see the attention he paid to the situation across the park. I heard one of the guys call out to the old woman, demanding her bag of groceries. Likely it was the only food the couple could afford for the next month. What would they eat if it was stolen?

"This. Life." I sighed. "I don't feel safe anywhere anymore, Ray. I don't know what I'm supposed to do. But this..." I gestured around the park, doing my best to ignore the old woman clutching her groceries to her chest. "This scares me."

"Marry me." I furrowed my brows and flashed him my left hand. "Way ahead of you." What did that have to do with anything? He smiled gently, shaking his head and lifting Avery out of the swing. "Not in June, babydoll. Marry me tomorrow. I'll keep you safe. I promise. I'll always keep you safe. I know it's backwards, but being married might be an extra layer of protection for you."

I was quiet, thinking about his offer. I had no doubt Ray would keep me safe. I just wasn't sure what lengths he would go to keep his word. I loved him, more than life itself, but was it worth it for him to risk himself, his family, for me?

Ray rested Avery on his hip, and grabbed me with his free hand. "Just think about it, okay? Don't say no right away. We're getting married in June anyway. Is it really such a big deal to move the wedding up a few weeks?"

I squeezed his hand in a silent response. He was right. But right now wasn't the time to discuss a wedding – a future – not when we were speed walking away from a mugging, the old lady's cries for help trailing after us on the street.

If I turned back now, tried to help her, it wouldn't end well for any of us. But it didn't stop the instinct ingrained so deeply inside me.

We made it back to Ray's apartment in record time and hurried up the stairs. We looked at each other, words needing to be said about what we had just witnessed and accepted as normal. It wasn't normal.

But this life had pushed us to be people we didn't recognize anymore.

Would our relationship survive that? Would our marriage? My thoughts were interrupted when a tiny hand grabbed at my coat, demanding my attention. "Meeeeeeeeela, I'm hungry."

I stuffed all the negative thoughts as far down as I could, giving the tiny girl a bright smile. "You're hungry, eh? Well, let's see what we can do about that."

Our afternoon was filled with keeping Avery entertained, and we had no time to talk, just the two of us.

Finally, just before sunset, Ray walked out of the bedroom, stretching his arms over his head. His lean figure wasn't altered by the shortages. Instead it only made his body harder. He walked around the living room and kitchen, turning on the random camping lanterns and flashlights we used to supplement the weak electricity. "She's down," Ray whispered, sitting next to me on the couch.

He lay back and I leaned into his body, desperate for comfort. He wrapped his arm around me, kissing me on the top of my head and stroking my hair lightly. "You should probably head home before it gets dark, unless you're staying the night."

"Nah, I need to check on Olivia. I'll leave in a minute." I watched the light streak into a prism of colors in the sky as day turned to twilight. "I love you, you know. Forever. No matter what."

"I know." His arm tightened around me. "Does this mean you'll marry me? Sooner, I mean."

"It means it isn't a no. Let me sleep on it, Ray. It's been a day." I'd marry the man in a garbage bag, and we both knew it. But my emotions were pulled a thousand ways by the weight of the day, and I didn't want to give him an answer swayed by anything other than love.

He kissed my head again. "Of course. You know I'm not going anywhere. I'll marry you tomorrow, June, in a thousand years. You're not getting rid of me that easily."

I laughed quietly, not wanting to disturb Avery. "Believe me, I know." Normally Ray would walk me home, but Avery was already asleep and he couldn't leave her.

So I left Ray sitting on the couch, with a promise to come back in the morning. We didn't bother promising to text or call. My phone still sat in my pocket, no bars to be had. I couldn't wrap my head around the idea that last night might have been the last time I'd ever get to use my cell phone. It was dusk, but not quite full dark, as I walked home, sticking to the busy roads and the sidewalks. *Just in case.*

Hopefully, Olivia would be awake and studying. Then I could bug her about all of my emotions from the day, and she would tell me how insane I was being.

Verbal sparring was our schtick, and it worked well for us. But just as I rounded the last corner to our apartment, I heard a commotion up ahead. I froze, instinct taking over, and pushed my back against the brick of the building behind me. Being out on the street after dark wasn't safe, but I needed to make sure there was a clear path to get into my apartment first. I slid along the wall, peeking around the corner to see what was happening.

I wasn't ready for what I saw. In front of our apartment, Olivia kicked and screamed as she was dragged into a parked car. Despite the obvious struggle, nobody stepped up to help her. How could they, without getting killed themselves?

I jumped around the corner, hiding behind our neighbor's garbage cans to try and figure out my next move.

One man held her back by her arms, keeping his distance. Likely, Olivia had already landed a solid blow or two on him. She had convinced me to take the self-defense classes with her, and hopefully they'd come in handy now. Another man was holding the door to the car open, and another sat in the driver's seat. Three men total. Not great odds.

But odds I needed to take. I shifted behind the garbage can, trying to get a better angle, and my foot kicked the metal with a hollow thunk. I couldn't breathe, wondering if they were going to catch me. None of the men looked my way, too caught up in Olivia's screams. But Olivia looked around, finally realizing who was hiding behind the cans.

Her eyes widened. She tossed a look behind her, at her captor dragging her into a silver minivan. There was absolutely no way for me to get to her without getting us both killed. We both knew it.

Fuck this world. Fuck what it had made me become.

First the old couple in the park, and now my best friend?

Fuck the Collapse.

"Run," she silently mouthed.

I shook my head, hair whipping into my eyes. *No.* I couldn't leave her. Not like this. I wasn't sure how to save her, but I had to try. I wouldn't be able to live with myself if I left her. Hot tears streamed uncontrollably down my face.

"Run," she mouthed again, eyes wild. "Mila, *run*!" This time she screamed loud, stopping the man holding her arms back in his tracks. I had never heard her sound this way before. Commanding. Frantic. *Scared.* "Run goddammit!"

For a split second I considered seeking refuge in our apartment. But if they had broken in to get Olivia, they would surely be back for me. The city wasn't safe.

So I ran in the opposite direction, as fast as my feet would carry me. I ran until the footfalls behind me turned into silence. I ran until the city turned into the suburbs, and the suburbs into farmland. I ran until my heartbeat stopped chanting Ray's and Olivia's names. I ran until the tears streaming down my face had dried, until I realized I was out in the middle of nowhere with no supplies, no support, and no hope. I ran, and I didn't look back, because I knew. Nobody could save me now.

TEN
Ray

I hadn't yet experienced a raid in my time as a Kingsnake. I supposed it was lucky, but really it was just laziness. The police weren't the "police" anymore so much as they were another gang. A group of guys banding together for self-protection and power, masquerading as good Samaritans.

There weren't women in the police force any longer. Some said it was because women were too afraid. We all knew the truth, though. The men wouldn't let women be a part of their club anymore. Of course, it was easier for them to play the upstanding citizen role, because even a decade after the Collapse, people still tended to think of the police as an organization that needed to be listened to. Ridiculous, really.

All the cops did was wield their strength to get what they needed, or just wanted, and if you didn't listen, you ended up lying in the street with a broken rib or a black eye.

Honestly, we were probably both dead either way. But it sounded nicer with a bit of hope attached. But we liked to play pretend, like we were still a functioning society. So Luke would pay them whatever he paid them (I doubted it was cash) and we would stay away from their wives and daughters. In exchange, they stayed away from us. For the most part.

Like tonight, for example. Someone had probably "tipped off" the cops to our whereabouts, and so the police would do their due diligence in checking out the motel. From what I was told from Snakes who'd been through previous raids, all the available brothers gathered the girls and hid them in plain sight in the basement.

The cops could find them if they wanted to, of course. But finding the girls meant more hassle for them. They didn't care about the Kingsnakes – the masks, the hoodies, the brotherhood – and they really didn't care about the girls either. But they had to pretend. So the police would come in, do a quick sweep, and then be on their way. A simple transaction that kept the other degenerate citizens satisfied.

I jogged up the stairs ahead of Luke, knocking on the doors as I passed. "Let's go, ladies! We have some surprise visitors tonight." When Luke darted into one of the rooms, I poked my head directly into Hannah's room. "Hannah, we've got the cops coming. We need to get you guys hidden." Hannah sprung out of bed, half asleep. "I'm coming."

Even the girls who didn't want to be here, like Hannah, knew to hide in a raid. You could never be too certain how the cops would assert their power, and the devil you knew was better than the devil you didn't.

I made sure I saw her getting ready to leave and then backed out of her room. Next was Mila. I took the key to her room out of my pocket. Most of the girls weren't locked in their rooms – unless they were a severe flight risk – but I had locked Mila inside for her own protection. Especially after she pissed off Tybalt this morning.

The lock clicked, and I swung the door open. Surprisingly, Mila was sitting on the edge of her bed, wide awake. "What's going on?" she asked. She was already awake again, fully dressed, shoes tied. "The cops are raiding us. We have to get to the basement." I crossed the room, offering her my hand. She stared at it blankly. "What does that have to do with me?" I sighed. I should've known this would be difficult.

The other girls were converging in the hallway, so I knew I only had a minute to convince her to get her ass downstairs. Easier said than done. "Mila, don't start with me. Not tonight. Trust me, you don't want to deal with the police."

She met my gaze with a steady glare. "Maybe I'd rather take my chances with them. At least they'd get me out of here, right?" I ground my teeth together, doing my best to not just drag her down the stairs with or without her consent. Because that would go over *so* well. "You haven't lived in the city for a long time, so I'm going to give you a piece of advice. Don't fuck with the police. They're as bad as, if not worse than, the Kingsnakes."

Mila tipped her head to the side, looking me up and down. She took in the mask, and the dark hoodie. The ripped jeans, and everything in between. "You mean as bad as *you*."

"Prospero, we need to get these girls down to the basement *now*." Luke's command echoed in Mila's room, and I scrubbed my hand over my face before looking back at the stubborn woman in front of me. "Mila," I snapped. "We need to go. Now." She held up her hands in defeat, getting to her feet. "Jesus, you don't need to be such a dick about it."

I rolled my eyes, making sure she joined the group in the hallway. She did, even though a scowl covered most of her pretty face, and her arms remained crossed.

Unimpressed. *Whatever.* I'd deal with her sass later. Luke met me at the top of the stairs. "You lead the group down to the basement. I'll take the rear. Hopefully Tybalt managed to wrangle the pregnant ones out of bed without too much problem."

I nodded, unable to say anything else lest I snapped about Mila or Tybalt. Neither of which would help me at the current moment. I took a quick count of the girls, noting Hannah's bright hair, and Mila's defensive stance in the group. At least they were both still present and accounted for. Turning, I made my way downstairs, the girls' footsteps following me as I kept a quick pace.

Another brother stood at the basement door, holding it open for us as I passed him with a nod. It only took a couple minutes in total, but my interaction with Mila had left me with a racing heart and a need for release. How could she be so stubborn, even during the apocalypse?

The brother holding the door open joined me in the basement, a small camp lantern lighting the small space. Luke had stayed upstairs to meet with the police after herding the girls downstairs. I looked around, taking note of my surroundings.

The basement wasn't the worst I had been in, but it wasn't great either. A couple of small windows faced the outside world, too high up to make for a comfortable escape, so they weren't barred. The girls stood mostly huddled together, and I realized I should probably do a quick count of them. I wasn't sure where Tybalt had taken the pregnant women, but they weren't down here, so there was probably another safe room just for them.

"Hey, brother?" I asked, watching half his face light up in the dim lantern. "Have you done a count?"

"Yep." His response was immediate, and reassured me. I didn't want to be responsible for any girls getting left in the cops' path. "Counted them as they came downstairs. All eighteen are here."

My heart froze. I knew who was missing without even looking at the group. "Excuse me?"

He frowned. "All eighteen are here, brother."

"You idiot," I muttered, squeezing the bridge of my nose. "There's nineteen of them. The new girl last night gave us nineteen."

"Oh, shit." His face fell, and I realized the brother in the basement with me was no more than a kid. "I swear I thought there were only eighteen."

"Yeah, well, you thought wrong."

110

I snatched the lantern out of his hands, scanning the group of girls. Sure enough, Mila's dark hair and frowning face were missing from the women we ushered into the basement. *Fucking hell.* I should've known.

I should've told Luke I would be at the back. I stuffed the lantern back into the brother's hands. "Stay here. Don't leave them for any reason until I come back down here."

"Okay. Uh... where... where are you going?" he stuttered. Shit. He really needed to grow a backbone if he was going to survive the Kingsnakes.

"I'm going to find the missing girl, from *your* mistake." It wasn't really his mistake, but I needed him scared enough to listen to what I said without question. And in the Kingsnakes, cockiness was power.

"You can't go up there!" He shook his head frantically. "The cops will be here any minute, and they only like to see Brother Brutus upstairs!" I paused with my foot on the bottom step, creaking beneath my weight.

"Either I go up there and find the girl, and possibly get myself in trouble, or they find the girl first and we're all screwed. Which would you rather?" The young brother was quiet, so I turned and jogged up the rest of the stairs.

Fucking Mila. I hoped she had at least hidden herself somewhere and wasn't attempting to take on the entire police force by herself. I wouldn't put it past her to try. I unlatched the door, peeking out into the common room.

So far it looked like just Luke was in the room, sitting at one of the old melamine tables. I stepped out into the light, closing the door behind me.

Luke turned with the sound of the latch, frowning at me through his mask. "What the hell are you doing up here?"

I met his eyes with a steady gaze. "One of the women is unaccounted for. We need to find her before the cops do."

Luke drummed his fingers on the tabletop. "It's my own damn fault for thinking we could handle more than fifteen women at a time. Sloppy of me, really." I didn't respond, seeing as he was mostly talking to himself. Finally he picked his head up to look at me again.

"Find her. Hide with her until the cops are gone, and then deal with her. We can't have loose ends like this and risk our entire livelihood. There's too much at stake."

Deal with her? Surely he couldn't mean to kill her. Right? "But, Luk– Brutus, it's..." Luke waved his hand in the air to dismiss me. "I don't care who it is. Whoever it is can't follow a simple direction for her own benefit. If she can't do that, why would I want her to bear our children?" He rolled his eyes, as if this idea was common knowledge.

"I'll send Tybalt after the cops leave. You can either take her body to the woods for the animals, or bury her in the back. I don't care which, just get it done. When the girls ask where she went, we can use her as an example to keep the rest of them in line. Fear works better than bullets on this lot." *He wanted me to kill Mila.*

How the hell was I going to get her out of this one? I couldn't very well blame the missing woman on someone else and watch them suffer a senseless death. But I wasn't about to kill Mila either. And with Tybalt watching my actions, there wouldn't be a chance for her to escape either.

Shit. "Why are you still standing there? Go find her." Luke shook his head, as if he couldn't comprehend my hesitation.

Which in all reality, he probably couldn't. To him, this was a calling as much as it was a business. And people who got in his way were unacceptable.

"Just thinking of where to start first. Good luck with the cops." I darted out of the room, leaving Luke sitting at his table – prince of a kingdom filled with snakes.

I wouldn't bother with the upstairs. Not yet at least. If I were Mila, I would be staying downstairs, somewhere close to an exit. The main floor was a mirror of the top floor where we kept the women, but usually the rooms were unoccupied.

We kept a couple made up in case a brother needed to crash, but other than that, they were empty. I opened the doors quickly, poking my head into each room, all the while keeping an ear out for the cops' arrival.

So far, they hadn't shown up, but each empty room I opened crushed me a little more. I was almost absolutely certain there was no way she could've snuck outside without someone seeing her.

I had two doors left, and I crossed my fingers as I opened each. No Mila. But the last bedroom held an unboarded window, and I raced over. She could've escaped easily. But beneath the window was nothing but fall mud, with no traces of footprints. Which meant either she hadn't noticed the window, or she had noticed and chosen not to escape.

I couldn't decide which was more likely.

Regardless, she wasn't in here, or outside.

So where the hell was she?

My heart was beating so loudly I could barely make out the sounds of the cops arriving, greeting Luke, and beginning their rounds. I was going to wring her neck when I found her, watching the color drain from her face.

She'd probably look at me and smile. Her cocky smile would forever be my undoing, Collapse or no Collapse. I would do whatever it took to make her smile at me like that forever. I just had to find her first.

I stepped out of the last room to see Luke round the corner – alone. He locked eyes with me, and nodded his head to the side. "And here are the main floor rooms. Usually it's just brothers who stay here if they're hard up," Luke announced to whoever was behind him. I took his signal to mean "get the hell out of here" and I ran around the corner as fast as I could, the voices of cops following me.

I was in the custodian's corridor now, a narrow hall lined with small closets and the laundry room. At the end of the hallway was another door to the kitchen. The closets were too small for Mila to hide in, but I opened them methodically anyways, listening to the voices of Luke and the cops catching up to me.

"Mila," I hissed, trying to stay calm and quiet. Nearly impossible given the situation. "Mila, this has gone on long enough." The cops were in one of the last bedrooms, and I knew I had only moments before they turned the corner. I flung open the door to the dark laundry room, the old washers and dryers judging me with their lone glass eyes. *Look what you've done*, they said. I ignored them, looking around the tight space for Mila.

"Mila," I whispered. "You have approximately two seconds before we get both our asses handed to us."

Nothing. Silence. The dead machines stared, and for a moment I thought maybe we both deserved this. The idea passed as quickly as it came – a second of weakness, brought on by circumstances neither of us merited. I turned to leave and scope out the kitchen in a last-ditch effort.

Just as my foot passed the threshold, I heard it. A small intake of breath, too big for a rodent. More like someone trying to breathe quietly. I stepped back into the room, letting the door swing shut behind me. As it closed, I could clearly see the space between the wall and the cupboard in the dim light. The space where Mila had wedged herself, giving me a look that would've rivaled the devil himself.

"You are in so much trouble," I muttered.

I wasn't sure if I was more relieved to find her alive, or pissed that she had tried to sneak off.

She tipped her chin up toward me, defiant and proud. "And what do you think you're going to do about it, Ray? You already told me you owned me for a month. Could it really get any worse than that?" Fury took over relief, simmering beneath the surface of my skin. "You have no idea, babydoll." I snatched her wrist, pulling her out from her hiding space, fully intent on dragging her back down the stairs to relative safety. But I heard the cops in the hallway before I got a chance to open the door, so instead of dragging Mila through the kitchen, I pushed her against the wall.

She gasped. "What the hell?" I pressed my hand against her mouth. "Make a single sound and we're both dead."

ELEVEN
Mila

Ray's hand pressed against my mouth. I couldn't breathe in the tight space. It was too dark, he was too close, and he needed to get his hand off my face. I shook my head, trying to dislodge his grip. He glared at me in the dim light.I looked into the face of Brutus. This time, those blue eyes didn't seem as charming. "You're coming with me."

"I'll take my hand off, *if* you promise to keep your mouth shut," he whispered, narrowing his eyes at me.

I nodded, desperate to taste even the stale air of the broken-down laundry room. He took his hand away, and I gasped, taking as big a breath as I possibly could. I steadied my breathing and my heart, then cocked my head to the side. I assumed by Ray's mannerisms that the cops were already here, and we were basically boxed in.

Contrary to whatever Ray was certainly thinking, my aim wasn't to be caught by the cops. Despite my snarky comments in my room, I knew not to trust the police.

I hadn't stayed alive this long on my own by being clueless. But I had hoped that by avoiding them for long enough, and with the rest of the Kingsnakes distracted by the raid, I might be able to sneak out. There'd been a chance. An open door on the main floor, and an unboarded window called me toward the sanctity of the forest. But at the last possible moment, just before I swung my leg over the shredded wooden pane, I thought about Ray's face. How crushed he would be if I fled again, without a word of goodbye.

The first time I left, I had only been concerned about my own survival. This time, it didn't seem right to only think about myself. This time, I knew what I was leaving him to survive alone, and my heart stuttered at the idea of what his punishment would be if I'd fled.

Would they blame him? Would it make this impossible situation even worse? I hated emotions, how they made me weak. You'd think the Collapse would've made us all feelingless zombies. Unfortunately not.

So instead of swinging my other leg out into the cool air, I had stepped back, running toward the kitchen. If I was lucky, I could make it back into the basement before anyone knew I was missing. And my next escape plan would include Ray.

Instead, Ray had rounded the corner before I could, and I darted into the small laundry room. Even though my heart had kept me here for him, his irritation when he found me only ignited mine. So now here we stood, chest to chest.

117

The rise and fall of his lungs echoed mine, the rhythm of my heart in tune with his own. Emotions were assholes, and one of these days they were going to get me killed.

I heard men talking just outside the room, and my eyes locked onto Ray. He nodded silently to me, pressing a finger to his lips, and grabbed my hip tightly with his free hand. They were pushing the door open, pressing the cool metal against my arm and Ray's back. Ray shuffled closer to me, every inch of his body touching mine. I couldn't breathe again, and I didn't think it was from nerves this time.

"Looks clear from here," an unfamiliar voice announced. If they took another step inside, if they let the door close, if they did any number of things, we'd be screwed. "It's kind of hard to do laundry without electricity." That was the voice of the brother who seemed to be in charge. Brutus? One of the other men laughed. "Don't I know it. My wife bitches about doing the laundry by hand every damn day. I told her she was lucky to even have clothes to wear."

Speaking of assholes. My body tensed, and Ray gripped my hip tighter, trying to get my attention. He shook his head, somehow knowing exactly what was going through my mind. I met his stare with a steady gaze of my own. I wasn't afraid of men. Not anymore. Not since I realized they were just as human as the rest of us.

Ray didn't look away. Not even when the door swung closed, or the voices slowly trailed away from the laundry room. He didn't step back either, his body pressed flush to mine. "What the hell were you thinking?" he hissed.

"Nothing? I didn't say anything."

I threw my shoulders back in an attempt to meet his stance, but it only succeeded in pushing me closer to him.

"You told me to stay quiet, and I was quiet."

"You know exactly what I mean."

I huffed. "I wasn't going to actually do anything."

"Yeah, okay," he scoffed. "We both know that's a lie."

I tried to turn away from him, but he had one arm next to my head, and the other still gripped tightly to my side. I pushed him back. "*We* don't know anything. I don't know how many times I can tell you there is no *we* anymore. And can you give me some damn space? I really don't need your cock digging into me right now." I meant it as a throwaway comment, but as soon as I said it, the energy between us shifted.

He didn't move, instead pushing my legs wider with his knee. "As soon as you walked back through those doors, there was a *we*."

"I didn't exactly walk through the doors, Ray. I was drugged and dragged." I rolled my eyes, but my voice caught when his fingertips dug into the top of my waistband.

"You can lie to yourself all you want, Mila. But don't lie to me. I know you too well. You don't want to be here, and neither do I." He snaked his fingers against my skin, slipping them into my pants. "That doesn't mean I haven't noticed how your body still reacts to mine. You still want me. Still need me. Still *crave* me." I didn't have enough air to respond, and I didn't know what words I would've gotten out with his hand finding its way between my legs. I knew I was wet, aching for his touch one more time.

119

Who knew how much time we really had together? But to admit I still craved him? No. I couldn't. Ray slipped his fingers between my soaked folds, giving me a crooked grin. I wanted to arch into his touch, to shift so his finger would be inside me, but I waited. He leaned forward, his lips against my ear. "I know you could've run, babydoll. So don't lie to me. Why'd you stay?"

Before I could answer, he sank his finger into my pussy. I sighed in pleasure, resting my head against the wall. Ray grabbed my chin with his free hand, forcing me to look at him once more. "Don't look away. You close your eyes, and I stop." I nodded, moaning as a second finger joined the first. He curled them up, stroking and pulsing, his palm grinding against my clit. My pleasure was building, my hips meeting his hand, my body desperate for release. "God, Ray," I groaned. "Let me come."

Ray didn't stop fucking me with his fingers, his palm still circling my throbbing clit. "Not yet. Not until you tell me why you didn't run when you had the chance." His hard cock pressed against my thigh, and I had no idea how he was able to keep his composure. His hand shifted into a faster rhythm, my body rocking in time as I rode the edge of an orgasm. My eyes flickered closed of their own accord, my body taking over for my mind. Ray slowed his ministrations.

"What did I say? Keep your eyes open. I want to watch you fall apart on my hand." I opened my eyes, and Ray smiled. His fingers resumed their tempo, and I panted as he watched carefully. "You ready to tell me why you didn't run?"

You, I mouthed.

He was an asshole, denying me my pleasure for an answer he already knew. He pushed a third finger inside me, and I arched my back, cursing. He ordered, "Out loud, babydoll. I want to hear the words out loud."

I gasped as all three fingers curled, stroking me just right. I was so close. "You," I spit out. "I couldn't leave you behind."

"Good girl," he whispered, leaning closer to me once more as he finger-fucked me harder. "Come for me." He kissed me for the first time since he had stepped foot into the laundry room, a kiss filled with unspoken desires and words we had long since forgotten. His tongue slipped between my lips at the same moment he pressed down on my clit, and I came. Hard. I cried out into his mouth, my pussy gripping his fingers as I trembled on his hand.

Ray kept his fingers moving, riding me through my orgasm. "You're so goddamn pretty when you come, Mila."

I rested my head against the wall again, trying to catch my breath. "What was all that about?"

"I already told you. You're mine for the month, and I plan on making the most of that time. Especially now that I know you want to be mine as well. I plan on using every last drop of you." I watched as he slipped his hand from my pants, putting his fingers into his mouth and sucking them clean.

I scoffed, even as my blood heated from the scene in front of me. "Where the hell did you get that idea?"

"You could've run. But you didn't." He shrugged. "The only logical explanation is you want to be mine. For now, at least."

"Or, I just felt bad leaving you in this hellhole all by yourself. Did you consider that possibility?"

Ray grinned at me, straightening my shirt with the ease of a protector. "Call it what you want, babydoll. But you're still here, and I just watched you fall apart on my fingers. And damn if you didn't look good doing it."

"Shut up," I muttered, but I couldn't help the smile growing on my lips. "Is it safe for us to go yet? I feel like this laundry room only has so much air left in it."

"Hold on." He pressed his ear against the door, his expression shifting from pleased to serious.

I leaned back, examining him in the faint light. I knew if I reached out, stroked his neck, he would curl into my touch. I knew he was still likely rock hard beneath his jeans, but he ignored it to get me off. I knew his left ribs were ticklish, a weak point I had often used to get my way.

I knew these things because I knew Ray, whether I wanted to or not. He was ingrained in me as deeply as one could be. And he was right. I had been able to leave him once, but leaving him twice was something my damaged soul couldn't afford. He continued. "I can't hear them, so I think we're okay. Let's give it another minute or so, then we should be good to get back into the basement."

"Okay." I chewed on my lip, trying to figure out how to phrase what I wanted to say. It wasn't the easiest thing to ask - Collapse or no Collapse.

"Ray?"

"Yeah?"

"Would you..." My tongue was heavy, tangled up on itself. But the words needed an escape, lest I live with regret for the rest of my life.

"Would you run away with me? Away from the city. I have a pretty good camp set up. It's not a solid house or anything, but it's not bad. And we could always find something else..." I trailed off, his silence making me nervous.

He sighed, an answer in itself. "It's okay. I know you have a lot to think about. And leaving the city is hard for anyone, no matter how screwed up it is now." It didn't mean my heart wasn't twisting in my chest at the idea of leaving him again. I knew I couldn't stay in the city forever, and I'd need to take the next opportunity I got. No hesitation next time.

"It's not that," Ray murmured. He reached out a hand to push my wild hair out of my face. "I have to think about my sisters too. Don't get me wrong, I want them out of the city. But leaving with two young girls means everything has to be planned down to the second. I can't afford any loose ends or mistakes."

"I get it." And I did. I understood his obligations. I was technically free and could escape whenever the odd chance arose. With Ray's sisters in mind, it convoluted a typically easy plan. We'd have to make sure they were close by, or go back and get them. Nothing could be spur of the moment.

He leaned forward, pressing a quick kiss to my forehead. "If the chance arises for all of us to leave, then I'll take it. No questions asked. But I can't risk my sisters' lives on a maybe."

I grabbed his hand without thinking, squeezing it tightly in a gesture reminiscent of our relationship a decade ago — not the one now. "Don't feel like you ever have to explain yourself to me. It's going to work out how it's going to work out, and neither of us have any control over that."

Ray laughed without humor. "Don't I know it." He poked his head out the door, opening it wider. "We're good."

I was just about to step into the hallway when Ray spoke again. "I do need you to agree to one thing for me."

He was out of the room, fully illuminated now, the edges of his curls peeking out from the bottom of his hoodie. "Anything."

"If something happens to me, if I..." He was silent, shaking off unwanted thoughts. "If something happens to me, or if I tell you to, I need you to take my sisters and run. We're still in the same apartment. Supplies are hidden in the loose floorboard, the one next to the bathroom. You take them, and you get them to safety no matter what."

I knew the floorboard he was talking about, because it was a hidey hole we had built together in university. Back then we used it to hide the good booze when we had parties, or a stash of weed if his landlord was coming by for an inspection. I assumed those weren't the kind of supplies he meant anymore. I nodded. "I'll do what I can. But we'll wait for you at the edge of the forest. For as long as we can."

Ray shook his head. "I need to know they're safe."

"They'll be safe." I crossed my arms. "But I'm not leaving the city again without trying to save the person telling me to run." He cocked his head to the side, watching me from behind his mask. "You mean... Olivia? Was she the one who told you to run?"

I was expecting him to ask, but hearing her name out loud gripped my heart like a vice. "I don't want to talk about it." I pushed past him, headed toward the kitchen.

"Where do you think you're going?" Ray grabbed my wrist before I could get the kitchen door opened.

"To the basement, like you told me to?" Ray in control really turned me on sometimes, but other times I just wanted to smack him. He shook his head, pulling me behind him as he headed for the door ahead of me. "Let me check first. It'll be easier to explain why I'm up here instead of you." I rolled my eyes but stayed silent. I knew he was right. I just didn't like that he was right.

He pushed open the swinging door, which protested with a gentle groan, before turning back to me. "All clear. Let's go." I followed Ray as he led me into the kitchen, through the opposite door, and toward the basement stairs once more. The common room was empty again, Brutus and the cops nowhere in sight. I dropped Ray's hand as soon as he opened the heavy wooden door, not wanting either of us to be questioned. Another brother I didn't recognize – this one a lot younger than the rest – stood at the bottom of the stairs with a camping lantern.

The yellow light lit up his mask in sharp angles and dark hollows that made me feel uncomfortable. "This her?" he called up the stairs to Ray. "This is her. I found her in the laundry room, no thanks to you." Ray's voice was firm and sharp – a contrast to the man who had commanded my orgasm only minutes previously.

My only problem was figuring out which was the act, and which was the real man. I hoped it was the one in the laundry room, but we had all changed so much since the Collapse. If he had to adapt to survive, how could I fault him?

"I'll deal with Brother Brutus after. That is, if you think you can manage getting all of the girls back to their rooms in one piece." We took the stairs one at a time, Ray's cautious footsteps echoing behind me in the gloom.

The brother muttered his assent, shoving me back with the rest of the girls. I righted myself, trying to blend in to the group once more. A hand caught my hair, pulling it away from my neck, and I found myself hoping it was Hannah. No such luck as I recognized the voice of Laura breathing into my ear. "You might fool the other brothers, but you don't fool me. I can smell the sex on you. But don't worry. Whatever game you're playing won't last long around here. I'll make sure of it." Before I could turn around to snap at her, my hair fell back in place, Laura lost to the darkness of the basement.

She couldn't really know, could she? She could assume, sure. But there was no way in hell she could know Ray's and my past. There was no way she could smell sex on me, because we hadn't *had* sex, but her bluff scared me regardless.

I tried to convince myself in the black of the basement. I repeated it to myself as one of the brothers opened the door, flooding us in light once more. I had almost convinced myself as I trailed the girls into the common room, when an arm grabbed me and pulled me out of line.

TWELVE

Ray

Luke caught me as I walked up the basement stairs, my eyes adjusting to the light. "Did you find her?"

"I did." If my answers were short enough, maybe he'd leave me alone, drop the situation altogether.

"Did you take care of her?" I frowned, looking away from him. "I took care of the situation." He pulled me over to one side of the room, out of earshot from the other brothers. "But did you take care of *her*?" I pressed my lips together.

The girls were making their way up from the basement now, tired and used. I refused to throw another one of the girls under the bus. Neither was I going to be the one signing Mila's death order.

But I wasn't sure how to get out of this situation.

"For fuck's sake, Ray. I told you to take care of her. She's a loose end." Luke pushed back his hood, running his hand through his hair in frustration. "It was the new girl, wasn't it? Mila. Your girl this month." I didn't want to give him the privilege of a response, but a muscle in my jaw ticked. I had only just got her back. Was the world really going to take her from me again?

"Shit, Ray. Wait right here. Don't fucking move." He stalked away from me, and I watched him pull Mila out of the line of girls. Her expression shifted from one of surprise, to anger, to resolve, all in the time it took for them to find their way back to me. By now the common room was empty, the brothers disappeared to make sure the girls were all tucked safely away upstairs. A pretense of protection.

Luke stared both of us down in the empty common room, as if expecting one of us to break. But together, neither of us could. "Who wants to explain the shitshow that just took place?" he asked. I chewed on the inside of my cheek, trying to figure out how best to explain what had happened without both of us ending up in backyard graves.

But Mila reached out, stopping just before she touched my hand, and spoke for both of us. "It was my fault, Brother Brutus. I wasn't paying attention, and I got lost on the way to the basement. I'm sorry. It won't happen again." Knowing Mila, I knew it was all an act. But to an outsider, it would seem as real and sincere as anything.

Luke's sharp gaze softened, if only briefly. "You expect me to believe that you just *got lost*?"

"Yes, sir. I stopped to tie my shoelace, and when I looked back up, everyone was gone. I tried to find my way, but I guess I took a wrong turn." I watched her nod out of the corner of my eye. Well, she was committed to the lie. The least I could do was back her up.

"It's true, brother. I caught her trying to find her way back to the basement. There were several open windows she could've escaped out of, but she didn't. I think we have a true believer here." Half a lie, half a truth. Both tasted bitter in my mouth. Mila had a chance to run, and stayed — for me.

But she'd never be a *true believer* in the Kingsnakes. Not in a million fucking years. Luke stuffed his hands in his pockets, watching us both. He thought he knew when I was lying and when I was telling the truth, and once upon a time he did. But now he only saw what I wanted him to see. A devoted Kingsnake, loyal to his brothers and the cause. And a girl – a vessel – who had made a silly mistake.

"If it was only an accident, I can give you one more chance, Mila. But if I find out any part of what either of you told me was a lie, there will be serious consequences for all involved. Otherwise known as a bullet to the head. *If* we had enough bullets to spare that month. "All true, Brother Brutus. I will take full responsibility for the girl until my month is up, and hopefully by then she will have proved her loyalty to the Kingsnakes."

"Very well." Luke turned, waving over a brother who stood at the bottom of the stairs. "Take Mila up to her room, and make sure she's locked in for the evening. We can't be too careful after today, can we?"

129

He turned back and grinned at me, but the underlying threat lacing his smile was easily apparent. Mila followed the brother up without a second glance backwards, her docile act enough to fool even me. I started to walk away, figuring I had pushed my luck enough today, but Luke spoke, stopping me before I got very far. "I know you want to protect the girls, Ray. But you need to remember they're just property. Vessels for us to use and fill. The Kingsnakes have a purpose to protect and provide for each other. If you get in the way of that, I won't hesitate to take you down."

I turned slightly back toward Luke, and pressed my hand against my chest. Pushing against the black snake embroidered in ink on my heart. A reminder of my sins, forever on my skin. "I know. And I need you to know I'm fully committed to the Kingsnakes. The girl truly was lost, and I don't see why she should be punished, when she might very well be a successful vessel." God, I wanted to be sick talking about Mila like that. As if she was no better than a body to be taken advantage of. "I'll do whatever it takes for the Kingsnakes to succeed."

"Will you?"

I faced Luke fully, who still stood in the corner with his hands in his pockets. "What do you mean by that?"

"Will you do whatever it takes for the Kingsnakes to succeed?" he repeated, walking toward me.

"I do my job, Luke. I hope you aren't questioning my loyalty." I didn't like the direction this conversation was headed, or the chill in Luke's voice.

He shrugged.

"All I know is you've been here for a decent amount of time, and none of your girls have gotten pregnant." My body went cold, my blood freezing in my veins. "Your point? Lots of the other brothers haven't been successful either."

"Lots of the other brothers haven't been protective of the girls the way you have. You seem to have a... connection with them." Luke sneered, as if the word was distasteful. "Most of your brothers treat the women as they should. Like empty vessels waiting to be blessed. You treat them as friends."

"What are you asking me for, *brother*?" I pulled myself up to my full height, meeting Luke toe to toe. At this moment, we weren't Kingsnake brothers, but high schoolers again.

"Proof."

I wasn't sure what I had been expecting him to say, but it wasn't that. "I'm sorry? Have you lost your *mind*?"

Luke's blue eyes flashed with annoyance. "I know we were friends once, but watch your tone with me, *brother*. And if you're really doing your job, proof shouldn't be difficult."

"I'm just baffled as to what kind of proof you're looking for. You want the bedsheets when I'm done? Wearing a condom seems a bit contradictory to me." Fucking *proof*. I shook my head. I couldn't understand Luke's train of thought a lot of the time, but this was excessive, even for him.

"No." His expression didn't shift, telling me exactly how serious he was. "Your next shift with Mila is tomorrow. I'll be joining you to make sure the Ceremony is carried out." I didn't think it was possible for my heart to sink any lower. And yet it did. "You can't be serious." Luke crossed his arms.

"Dead." He turned and walked away, effectively dismissing me. "Besides, it's not as if you're making love to the girl." Yeah. It was just fucking. Or at least that's what I told myself. Only now, it'd be fucking with an audience.

The night passed in a restless sleep – if I slept at all. It sure didn't feel like it. My mind kept focusing on what Mila's reaction would be when she realized what was happening. We didn't have a choice if we wanted to live. And if I knew Mila as well as I thought I did, she'd do whatever it took to survive. I just wasn't sure how much of my soul I would have to sacrifice. Maybe I had made a mistake, joining the Kingsnakes. Maybe it would've been better to end up homeless and penniless, instead of permanently marked by this damned gang.

But when I looked at my sisters, I knew I had made the right call. I might have paid the price with my own heart, but at least these two young girls were protected from the worst of the world. For now at least. I was unfocused during our morning routine, exhausted from my sleepless night.

Avery had to call me three or four times to get my attention. We sat at the scuffed dining room table, working through an old poetry book I had found in the motel. Every other morning we devoted ourselves to English – grammar, reading, and writing. The alternating mornings were math.

And in the afternoons, after lunch, we would work on basic survival skills. So many of us were caught off guard after the Collapse, ill-prepared to be self-sustainable.

I refused to let my sisters end up helpless. I wanted them to be able to rely on themselves, and each other, if anything were to happen to me. Our day dragged on, the old watch on my wrist making each minute feel like an hour.

But eventually the sun began to set, and I pressed a kiss to each of the girls' foreheads and told them goodnight. I was a man walking to the gallows, a prisoner attending his own execution. Each creak of the rickety fire escape reminded me of where I was going, and what I was about to do. I hoped like hell Mila would forgive me.

I knocked on the door to the motel, opening to reveal Tybalt's scowling face. Thankfully no excuses were necessary this time. "Brother Prospero." I met his stare with an intimidating glare. The Kingsnakes responded to confidence, something I had quickly picked up. "Brother Tybalt. I hope the day was... uneventful for you."

He didn't respond, simply turned away and left me to enter the motel on my own. I locked the door behind me and found my way to the common room. Ceremony nights were fairly lax on timing, as long as the brothers checked in and out with Luke or one of the other senior Kingsnakes. I had dragged my feet leaving the apartment, so I wasn't surprised that only Luke remained in the common room after Tybalt disappeared upstairs.

"Brother Prospero," Luke greeted me. "Are you ready for your Ceremony?" I sucked in a breath through my teeth.

"As I'll ever be." Climbing the stairs to the bedrooms felt like it took years, each step as impossible as Everest. But eventually we found ourselves in front of Mila's room. Luke tipped his head, a soft smile ghosting across his lips. "After you." I gathered all my strength and opened Mila's door.

She sat on the edge of her bed, her camping lantern efficiently lighting the small space. When she saw me, she smiled. But when she saw who was behind me, her smile dropped completely. "Brother Brutus?" she questioned.

"Hello, Mila. I hope you don't mind, but I've asked Brother Prospero if I can be a silent observer during your Ceremony tonight. I'm sure you understand we need to see how loyal you both are to the Kingsnakes after your little *mishap* yesterday." He smiled, but his sickly charm couldn't hide the venom. He enjoyed toying with us.

Mila frowned. "You... you want to watch us have sex?"

Luke laughed, the artificial sound filling Mila's small bedroom. "As I said to Brother Prospero, it's not as if you two are making love on your wedding night." I cringed at the mention of a wedding night – a night I had long anticipated, but would never get to experience. Mila was quiet, thinking for a moment before she responded. "If I decline?"

Luke stopped laughing. "Then you'll no longer be welcome here. Of course, we can't let you go back into the world freely, either." The underlying threat was clear as day.

You'll let me watch, or I'll kill you.

"Fine." Mila flung herself back on the bed. "Let's get this over with then." This was going to be ten times more difficult than I had originally anticipated.

Luke shut the door, standing in the corner with his arms crossed. He was seriously just going to stand there and watch me fuck her. When I stared at him, and he did nothing but stare back, I had my answer.

I turned toward Mila, doing my best to ignore Luke's eyes drilling holes into my back. I stripped off my sweater and T-shirt, being careful to leave my mask in place.

When I crawled over Mila to straddle her on the bed, her eyes trailed over my bare chest, taking in the snake tattoo reminding everyone of who I was. Her gaze climbed, meeting my eyes behind my bone mask. A question reflected back at me, unspoken, but hanging in the air just the same. I unbuttoned my jeans, pushing them over my hips, and did the same for Mila as she lay there, silently watching me.

I left her shirt on. Luke could force us to do this while he watched, but he didn't need to see everything. I nudged her legs wider with my knees, resting a hand on either side of her face. "Look at me, Mila," I whispered. My words were barely more than a breath, enough for her to hear, but not loud enough Luke would be able to discern them from across the room. "Look at me." Her brilliant green eyes met mine, wary and unsure.

"Do you trust me?" I wouldn't blame her if she didn't. Look where she was, what I was making her do. But she nodded, never once taking her eyes off me. Luke's presence lurked behind me, and I did my best to ignore him, putting him out of my mind. I had to, for Mila's sake. I couldn't say much else with Luke watching so closely, but I didn't need words to communicate with Mila. I never had.

We had spent nights in her bed, Olivia on the other side of the thin dorm wall, having entire conversations without speaking once. If only a university roommate was our only problem now... *It's just you and me, babydoll*, I pleaded silently. *Keep your eyes on me. Nothing else matters right now. Just you and me.* I couldn't be certain, but I was sure she knew what I meant.

Just you and me, she would say, if she could. There was no way she would've admitted such a thing if we weren't in this situation, but everything was different now. I reached between her legs, not expecting to find her ready for me, and cursing when I found she was wet all the same. *You and me*, I thought, spreading her desire around her pussy, fitting myself to her entrance.

Mila looked up at me, putting her hand directly on top of my tattoo and gave me the smallest of nods. *It's okay*, her green eyes reassured. *It's okay.*

It wasn't, and I wasn't sure it'd ever be okay again. But with her blessing, I pushed myself inside her. It felt wrong, to enjoy the feeling of her tight pussy while we were being forced to have sex, but I couldn't control my groan. Mila's eyes fluttered back, even though she was silent. I knew she was enjoying it, but she wouldn't give Luke an ounce of satisfaction, either.

My tough fucking girl. The one who laughed in the face of danger, and reassured me when I was doing terrible things. I would never deserve her, not in a thousand lifetimes.

But this? Making her feel good, forgetting the messed-up world we inhabited?

That I could do, even if it was just for a moment. I began to thrust inside her, watching her face for cues of what she needed from me. I drove myself deeper, her mouth curving into a perfect "o" of pleasure. Her hips rose up to meet mine, and together we found our tempo, just as we had always done. I could imagine the noises she would make if it were just the two of us. The small cries I would swallow with my kisses, and the curses of passion as her orgasm built with each thrust of my cock. I could imagine it so clearly, in tune with the way her body responded to mine, and eventually everything began to slip away.

I forgot Luke was watching me fuck Mila.

I forgot the motel, the Ceremony.

It was just us, our bodies moving as one. I locked my eyes onto hers, her pussy beginning to clamp tightly around me. I knew she was close. I nodded, pistoning my cock faster and grinding my hips against hers, until I felt her silent release shake through her. Watching her in quiet pleasure was enough to send me over the edge, my orgasm loud enough for the both of us as I cried out and filled her. There was nothing but Mila, myself, and our heavy breaths as we came down from our high.

Behind me, Luke clapped, bringing me back to reality. "I don't know what I had expected, but it seems you're both true believers. I wouldn't be surprised if Mila moves to the other side of the hotel at the end of the month." He gave both of us broad smiles, and turned to leave the room. "I'll be waiting for you outside, Brother Prospero. I'll give you both a minute to get cleaned up. Good night, Mila."

How generous, I thought. The door closed behind him, and I immediately faced Mila. "I am *so* sorry," I whispered. She shook her head, frowning. "Don't apologize, Ray. This world... it isn't for the weak. We all have to do terrible things to stay alive." I sighed, buttoning my pants and pulling my shirt back over my head. "All the same, I'm still sorry."

"I know." Mila reached over, squeezing my hand briefly. "I know you are. And I promise you it's going to be okay." Her touch reassured me, like old times. It was the two of us against the world, and when we were together, anything was possible. I sighed, squeezing her hand back and getting to my feet. Our time was limited with Luke outside the door.

"I hope you're right."

"I'm always right," she whispered after me, and I couldn't help the smile that spread across my lips. I turned back, shaking my head at her, before I opened the door and joined Luke in the hallway. We didn't speak until we reached the top of the stairs, having to go down them single file.

Luke descended first, clapping a hand on my shoulder as he passed me. "You're a good man, Ray. I'm proud to call you my brother." I didn't respond. I wasn't sure what emotion was churning my stomach, but I knew for a fact it wasn't pride. And I definitely knew I wasn't a good man.

That man had died the minute I went looking for the Kingsnakes.

THIRTEEN
Mila

The days bled into each other, blurring into weeks. The Kingsnakes ran a tight ship, and weaknesses for a planned escape were few. The only measure of time I had was Ray coming every other night.

Our relationship had shifted since that evening with Luke, and we had both felt it. I didn't blame him – couldn't blame him – for what had happened.

But unspoken feelings still swirled around us whenever we were together.

Did I still love him?

To me, love was the only explanation I had for being a willing participant in what felt like a united front in the face of evil. A mutual surrender for the safety of not only us, but his sisters as well.

Sometimes we had sex.

Sometimes we talked.

Sometimes we dreamed.

Ray had keys to my door, but escape wouldn't be as simple as opening the front door and running down the street. We would need keys for the main doors. I was a commodity, one the Kingsnakes would be loath to lose. And Ray was a bonded member. They wouldn't let him go without a fight.

Either of us leaving without a carefully orchestrated plan could have dire consequences for both us and Ray's sisters. It didn't stop us from imagining a world outside of the motel, though.

"Is it hard?" he asked one night, both of us lying on my small bed. Moonlight streamed through the slats in the window, and my camp lantern illuminated the rest of the room in a warm glow.

"Is what hard?" His head rested on my chest, and I tangled my fingers through his curls. We never spoke about what had changed that night. But our relationship had evolved, throwing us back to a level of comfort we had last experienced as young, naive university students.

Maybe it was destiny. Or maybe it was because we found each other on the same team, fighting against the same evil.

Ray lifted his head, propping himself up on his elbows. "Living outside the city. Foraging. Rationing the supplies you do bring out there." I brushed a stray lock of hair out of his face, a smile ghosting across his lips with the gentle touch. "It was at first. The loneliness was the worst." I sighed, remembering my first few months in the woods.

After a few cold and hungry nights huddled against a tree, I had braved the trip back to the city, intending to acquire anything useful I could carry on my back. I looked over my shoulder with every step, hoping to see Olivia around every corner. No such luck. I didn't trust the trip further into the city to shop at the large grocery store, so instead I hit up the gas station on the edge of town.

The windows were haphazardly boarded up, and a shotgun sat on the counter in front of the clerk. I paid for my protein bars and ran, not waiting around to see why the shotgun was there. "I thought about stopping by your apartment the first night I came back. To explain. But I got halfway there, and saw two men in hoodies at the corner. A van was waiting for them on the street. I turned around, and there were three more across the street, following another elderly couple. It was almost like a completely different world to the one I had left only days earlier. The woods... the woods seemed like the safer option." I could still taste the fear, a metallic flavor on my tongue, as I turned and hurried back to the gas station.

Away from the life I'd always known. Ray frowned. "But why didn't you call me? Leave me a note? I would've come and found you. I could've protected you, Mila. I could've offered you a safe place to stay. Maybe all of this would've been completely different."

"And maybe it all would've been completely worse." I shook my head. I wasn't sure if I could explain the complete and utter fear I felt coming back to a city I had once known like the back of my hand.

"If I had gone to your apartment, and you weren't there, I don't think I would've... I don't think I would've been able to handle it. Not after Olivia."

The crease between his brows smoothed out, and he nodded. "Easier to pretend you knew I was safe."

"Exactly." It hadn't made leaving any less difficult. But I did it. And I did it time and time again, as the gas station closed, and then the corner store. Until all that was left was the grocery store, a thick shell around my once-delicate soul, and a faint memory of the way Ray smiled at me. "Besides, how would I have gotten word to you? My phone was already long dead. We both know leaving a note with anyone would've been a joke. I had to make a choice. A difficult one. But a choice that allowed me to survive."

Ray watched me, tracing circles on the inside of my wrist. "What happened to Olivia?" I knew this was coming. He hadn't asked me since that day in the laundry room, but I knew he'd ask me again eventually. "I was careful going home that day, but when I got to my street, I saw these men forcing her into a van. I was trying to figure out how to help when she saw me." That exact moment haunted me for months. Her blonde hair whipping every which way as she fought off her kidnappers. The way she had screamed at me. "She told me to run. She risked herself for me, Ray. I didn't know what else to do besides run."

"So you weren't just pulling a runaway bride then." He grinned, lighting up his entire face. I laughed, trying to keep quiet so as to not alert any other brothers who might still be on the floor.

"No. Definitely not. Is that what you thought all this time?"

"You really think I'm that whipped?" Ray winked, and checked the watch on his wrist. I hadn't seen a watch in years, and I had no idea how he had managed to keep the thing alive for so long. But with Ray, anything was possible. "I should get going. Avery won't sleep until I'm home."

He got to his feet, and I crossed my legs as I sat up. "She's a good kid, Ray. I know you're doing a good job with her. With both of them."

"Thanks." He was quiet, putting his hoodie back on and pulling his mask over his face. Transformation complete, he looked down at me. "They both know basic survival skills. Shelters, foraging, fires. That sort of thing. If the time comes, they won't be a burden on you. I've taught them both to carry their own weight."

I sat up straighter. "Don't."

Ray paused with his hand on the door knob. "Don't what?"

"Don't act like you won't be there with us. If we're escaping, we're doing it together. *All* of us." I wasn't leaving anyone behind this time.

Ray gave me a sad smile, his eyes hidden in the shadows of his mask. "Unfortunately, in this world, we can't always get what we want." He stepped outside, leaving me alone in my room with his words echoing in my ears.

For the most part, I tried to avoid the other girls. It wasn't too hard. I was used to being alone, so keeping myself in my room wasn't difficult. But I couldn't live in my room permanently.

The Kingsnakes managed to cut off water to the individual rooms, meaning the only showers were down in the useless gym. Communal style – simpler to keep an eye on all of us. Meals were usually shared for ease.

After Ray's mournful warning kept me up all night, I knocked on Hannah's door first thing in the morning. Normally Hannah came and woke me up early so we could eat breakfast before the other girls woke up. But this morning she hadn't come to my room yet, and the sun was already beaming through my slatted window.

"Hannah?" I called. Silence for a minute, and then I heard her soft footsteps shuffling to the door. "Hey," she greeted me, still half asleep. Her long red hair was askew every which way, and she looked absolutely exhausted. "Sorry, I must have slept in."

"No, it's totally fine." I shook my head, examining her carefully. "You feeling okay? I can always get one of the brothers if you think you need medicine." I didn't want to have to get one of the Kingsnakes for help, but disease was inevitable after the Collapse. If Hannah was coming down with something we needed to catch it now, before it had a chance to spread.

"No. Don't get one of them. I'm just tired." She sighed, grabbing her ratty cardigan from her bed and pulling it over her frail shoulders.

"I just never really saw my life ending up this way. I guess it's really getting to me lately." I offered her a smile. I understood the feeling more than I would ever be able to convey. How did you explain the need to survive in a world that just wanted to destroy you? "I don't think any of us did. Your brother... is he treating you okay?" Hannah shrugged.

"As well as I could hope for, I guess. Come on. Let's get some breakfast before the Snake Charmers eat it all." I followed her downstairs to the kitchen, past the nameless, faceless brother on duty. I had learned to pretend like they were no more than decoration. It was a child's game, really. If I didn't notice them, they wouldn't notice me.

Chatter drifted out the door, more voices than during our normal breakfast time. I tried to hide my grimace. As much as I did my best to ignore the Kingsnakes, I also did my best to avoid the other girls.

Especially Laura. The girl had it out for me, but as long as I stayed out of her way, there was nothing she could really do. For now.

From the sounds of it, Laura was holding court in the kitchen. I had also learned most of the brothers let the drama play out unless it came to physical blows – free entertainment for them. I really didn't want to get involved in whatever was happening this morning, but my stomach was growling, and Hannah was already halfway in the door.

Laura clocked us as soon as we walked in, turning away from the poor girl she had been berating for some reason or another. "Well if it isn't the slut and her best friend, Little Orphan Annie."

I rolled my eyes, turning away from Laura's sharp glare and reaching into the cupboard that held food stuff. The Kingsnakes hadn't been too successful in their supply runs lately, so our choices were limited. Protein bars, mystery meat jerky, and some stale crackers were the only things on the menu.

"Save it for someone who cares, Laura." I grabbed two protein bars, stuffing one into Hannah's hand, and opening the other for myself. I wanted to go back and hide in my room, but I wasn't about to leave Hannah here alone to face the sharks.

Laura crossed her arms, still dressed in her tight-fitting club dress that had seen better days. Sparkles were missing in whole chunks, leaving her looking like a dying star. And even before noon, she teetered in her high heels. "I'm not stupid, Mila. I know exactly what's going on with you and Brother Prospero."

My chest tightened. I forced myself to chew the bite of protein bar before I answered. There was no way she could *really* know what was going on between us. "Well I'd hope you'd know how babies are made at this point."

Muffled laughter scattered across the kitchen, and Laura's glare grew deadly. "You know exactly what I mean. And if you don't start showing me the respect I deserve, I have no problem going to Brother Brutus with my information."

I needed to figure out what "information" she thought she had. Either that or intimidate the hell out of her so she wouldn't say a word. Right now, intimidation seemed the best course of action.

"Sorry, and what respect would that be? Respect because you're still wearing heels ten years into the apocalypse? Respect because you think you're better than the other girls here, even though we're all captives?" Hannah was pulling at my sleeve, silently trying to get me to stop, but fear was fueling my fury at this point. "Face it, Laura. We're all fucked, in more ways than one."

Laura tossed her hair over her shoulder, her face turning redder by the second. "How dare you think we're equals. As if I could ever be on the same level as you."

"Well, let's see." I crumpled the wrapper in my hand and stalked across the kitchen. "We're both getting screwed by a nameless, faceless man in hopes we wind up pregnant with his baby. And if said pregnancy happens, our baby will be taken away from us, sold for goods to the highest bidder to keep us alive. Seeing any differences so far?"

She narrowed her eyes to slits and crossed her arms, but remained silent. I knew I was hitting pressure points she'd rather ignore. So I kept digging. "We don't get a say in who fucks us either. Meaning I didn't choose Brother Prospero, and you didn't choose whoever got stuck with your annoying ass this month."

"You really want to go down this path with me?" Laura snapped. "I can make your life a living hell."

I threw my arms out to the side, looking around the crumbling kitchen and the waiflike girls standing in it. "Go ahead. You've been threatening that since the second day I walked in here. The first day you were too busy welcoming me to hell."

Laura huffed and stomped her heel on the ground. "Fine. If you want to test me, let's see how you feel about this." She pushed past me, out of the kitchen. I followed her close behind."What the hell do you think you're doing?" I grabbed her wrist. She turned back to me with a sneer.

"What does it look like I'm doing? I told you I would share your little secret, and you wanted to push the matter. The consequences are your own fault." She wrenched her wrist out of my grasp and stormed over to the brother who was flipping through a tattered horror book. Ironic, really. As if there wasn't enough horror in the world as it was.

"Brother, I have something you really need to know."

The Kingsnake on duty was one of the young ones. He snapped his head up, seemingly surprised a girl dared to directly address him. "Um, okay?"

Ignoring the rest of the girls piling out of the kitchen behind us, I focused on the brother. "It's nothing you haven't heard before, brother. Ignore her."

"Don't listen to Mila. She's just afraid of getting in trouble." Laura smirked at me over her shoulder.

"You're kidding me, right?" I laughed, trying to make it as realistic as I could.

"Unless you'd like to tell him yourself?" she offered, as if handing a child a piece of candy.

The brother looked back and forth between the two of us, complete bewilderment apparent in his eyes behind the mask. Apparently this young Kingsnake hadn't grown up with sisters. Poor thing probably never interacted with a girl before the world went to shit.

He raised both hands in the air, signaling for us to stop. "Okay, okay, look. I've been warned about you two causing shit before. I'm too tired to deal with it. So you are going back to your room." He pointed at Laura, who frowned. "And you are going back to your room. Both of you are going to stay there until Brother Brutus can deal with you himself."

I tried to speak up to complain, but Laura was speaking just as loudly, bemoaning she was merely looking out for the Kingsnakes.

"Both of you can shut up," the brother snarled. "I don't have the patience to deal with your petty bullshit. Your rooms. Now!" Both of us would've snapped back, tempers strained, if another brother hadn't arrived at that moment. He glared at us, flipping up his hoodie enough for us to see the pistol sticking out of his pants. "What's the problem in here?" I glared at Laura, and she sneered back at me. Neither of us were used to backing down, but survival trumped all, and a gun wasn't something I was going to take a risk with. So we both shut up, and trudged up the stairs.

The first Kingsnake followed us up, Laura leading the way toppling in her too-high heels, me trailing behind shooting daggers at her back. I still wasn't sure what information she thought she was going to share, and now I would have no way to find out until she told Brutus in person. I might very well be dead – especially after the shitshow of the raid. Maybe I'd be able to sneak into her room, and at least figure out what she knew. Or thought she knew.

Laura stomped into her room, slamming the door shut, and the brother quickly locked it behind her.

He turned back to me with a shrug. "Sorry not sorry. You'll both be locked in until Brother Brutus arrives."

Well there went that plan. I stormed into my own room, flinging the door shut. The lock clicked, and the brother's steps trailed away. I had done *so* well avoiding all the girls, and all the drama, just like Ray had asked. But I just couldn't help opening my goddamn mouth when I should've been blending into the background.

Too bad I had never been much of a side character. I flopped on my bed, dreading the hours until evening. How would I explain this to Ray? He was going to be pissed.

The day dragged as I lay on my bed, watching the sunlight shift through the gaps in my window. I tried to think of any which way to escape my trial, to no avail. Eventually, the blue sky started to streak with orange and pink, and I turned on my lantern.

It wasn't long before a key clicked in my lock again, and lucky for me it was my favorite brother, Brother Dogberry, poking his head into my bedroom. "Let's go, new girl. I heard you were causing trouble again." I rolled my eyes, being careful to not let him see. "Not exactly."

"Good thing I like a girl with a bit of fire," he murmured as I passed him in the doorway. I did my best not to gag. I tried to walk ahead of him, but he forcefully gripped my bicep. "Not so fast, sparky. I was given explicit instructions to take you directly to Brother Brutus's office, and I am not about to let him down." Dogberry pulled me closer, leaning his head against my neck and breathing deeply. "You better not let anyone else see you," I warned.

"I don't think Brother Prospero takes kindly to sharing." At least, I hoped he didn't. Dogberry chuckled, and I pulled my arm a bit looser from his firm grasp. "The Choosing is in two days, so you might as well accept that you'll be mine for the next month. Think of the fun we'll have."

No thank you. I did my best to ignore Dogberry's comments as we walked downstairs. He led me to a small room next to the kitchen. Brother Brutus sat behind an aged desk. Laura stood on the other side of it, grinning at me as I entered.

"Thank you, Brother Dogberry. You can leave us now." Brutus dismissed Dogberry with an ease that would've made me smile if I were anywhere else. But being alone with Laura and Brutus only made my heart pound.

Dogberry sighed behind me, and the door closed, leaving just the three of us. This wasn't good. Brutus sat back in his office chair, which no longer had wheels but most likely did at some point. Now it just sat behind the desk on its thin legs.

I looked everywhere except into Brutus's piercing blue eyes. I was certain if I stared directly at them, the truth would come spilling out of my mouth. Instead I scoped out his office, a room that remained locked unless he was at the motel. There was a window that wasn't boarded up, the tackiest orange curtains framing the dusty glass. Stacks of newspapers surrounded his desk. Some people collected baseball cards to make them feel normal.

Obviously Brutus collected newspapers. It explained the newspaper decor in the common room. But the biggest shame of all was behind him – shelves and shelves of books.

What a waste, to surround the office of an oaf like him. Those books deserved a better home.

"Laura, you said you have some kind of information about Brother Prospero and Mila to share with me?" I wouldn't look. Couldn't look. As long as I kept my gaze separate, I was safe. Maybe I would even recognize one or two of the books on the shelf. A girl could dream, right?

Beside me, Laura cleared her throat. I could practically feel the victory leaching off her skin into the room. This was it, the moment of truth. "I have reason to believe Brother Prospero and Mila are engaged in a relationship outside of the Kingsnakes' arrangement."

FOURTEEN

Ray

It seemed like I was constantly running late to the motel. I used to be on time, conscious of appearances.

Now, I didn't care about anything except my sisters and Mila. And today, I had an important mission to accomplish before I went and saw Mila. After I had said goodbye to my sisters, making sure they were occupied in the small kitchen, I snuck into the hallway. I grabbed my supply bags from their hiding place under the loose floorboard, and left.

Before I had entered the motel, I snuck around the back where an old shed stood. Once it might've stored a lawnmower, maybe a snowblower.

Now it would hold the supplies that would keep my sisters and Mila alive while they escaped.

I had devised a plan.

A plan I was fairly certain would work, so long as everything fell into place. I was excited to tell Mila about it, to see her face light up when she realized there was a chance we might all get to be happy. *Free.*

I pulled my mask over my face and stepped into the motel, ignoring Brother Dogberry's gloating expression as he unlocked the door for me. He didn't say anything, but I could feel his grin at my back the entire length of the hallway. Finally I turned and scowled at him.

"Do you have a problem?"

"No." His slimy smile grew and I wanted to punch his teeth out. It probably wouldn't have taken much, as brown and rotten as they were. "Then why are you smiling like a goddamn clown?" Dogberry pissed me off.

It had only gotten worse since the situation with Mila, but I still attempted to contain my irritation. Dogberry shrugged. "Seems like your girl is a troublemaker. She's in the office with Brother Brutus right now." I closed my eyes and sighed. "You're fucking kidding me."

"Nope," Dogberry chirped. "God, I bet she's a fun one. I can't wait for a turn with her."

"Shut your goddamn mouth, or I'll shut it for you." Dogberry was headed in the right direction for a black eye, and I would have no problem explaining to Luke exactly why he deserved it. But first I had to deal with Mila. "Don't you have somewhere you need to be?" I ignored whatever weak excuse was going to come out of his mouth next, and marched across the common room toward Luke's office.

I knocked on the door, not bothering to wait for an acknowledgement before I entered. "If it isn't the man of the hour," Luke greeted me. He was holding court behind his desk, a pleased-looking Laura on one side of me and a pissed Mila on the other.

"Laura here was just telling me she has reason to believe you and Mila have a relationship outside of the Ceremonies. I'd love to hear your side of it."

Well, shit. I was almost positive we hadn't been caught. I'd been careful, covering my tracks. We barely acknowledged each other in public. So I decided to play it off, laughing.

"Oh, yeah? And what makes her think that?"

Laura's smile dropped. She had obviously thought she was going to catch us off guard, tripping us up enough that we'd play into her hand. Maybe she had nothing after all. Luke tipped his head toward Laura. "Your evidence?"

Her eyes widened slightly. "Uh... I saw you two come back into the basement together after the raid. God only knows what you were up to while you were gone."

"You mean when Mila got lost, and I had to make sure we were hidden from the cops?" I crossed my arms over my chest, looking at Luke as if this was the most ridiculous thing I had ever heard. I ignored my racing pulse, convincing myself I was in control of this situation.

Not Laura. Not Luke. *Me*.

"Anything else you'd like to add?" Luke smirked at me as he addressed Laura, and I wanted to breathe a sigh of relief. He was just toying with her, playing the game.

"Mila just seems way too comfortable here for a girl in her first month." Laura huffed, and I half expected her to stomp her high-heeled foot. This time, my laugh wasn't faked.

"I'm sorry, but the basis of your argument is that Mila is too comfortable here?" Her weak argument was my saving grace. "Did you ever consider that she's just grateful for a roof over her head and food to eat?"

Even Luke's smile grew broad. "You have to admit the absurdity of such a statement, Laura. Isn't that what anyone could hope for? To be immediately comfortable with the cause?" Mila remained silent. I wanted to reach out to her, to look her in the eyes, and ask her what she was thinking. I wanted to kiss her troubles away, one by one. What was running through that beautiful mind of hers?

"But... but... but..." Laura stammered. I knew girls like Laura, before the Collapse. Girls who were used to getting their own way. Girls who broke when anything differed from the status quo.

Luke narrowed his eyes. "Laura, you're dismissed. Next time you have concerns, make sure they're valid. I don't need my time wasted." I offered Laura a small wave, and she glared at me as she walked by.

Bitch. Luke turned his attention to Mila, who still hadn't looked at me or spoken. "Mila, you're dismissed as well. You can wait for Brother Prospero in your room."

I watched her out of the corner of my eye as she nodded and raced out of the room. I really needed to talk to her. But Luke was looking at me expectantly, and I knew I needed to finish this conversation first.

"Please tell me you believed none of that Snake Charmer's story." I rolled my eyes for emphasis, trying to play up exactly how absurd I thought Laura's explanations were. Little did she know, she was more right than she realized.

"Of course not." Luke laughed. "I saw both yours and Mila's dedication to the cause earlier this month. Besides, the Choosing is in two nights. Even if there was something extracurricular going on between you two, it would have to end then. I can't imagine any man being okay with his female being impregnated by someone else."

The fucking Choosing. I thought back to Dogberry's comments. How had I forgotten how close the Choosing was? My blood ran cold, imagining another man's hands running up Mila's smooth skin. I wanted to rip my imaginary enemy limb from limb for touching her lips, or sinking inside her warm pussy. Mila was *mine*. "True."

"I don't have anything to be worried about, do I, Ray?" Luke eyed me, a smile on his face. But I couldn't help feeling like the smile was a front, hiding a truth he didn't want to share with me. "Absolutely not. I'm fully committed to the Kingsnakes." Another lie. Another sin. When would it end?

"Good." Luke's smile grew. "Then you, too, are dismissed. Try and stay out of trouble, all right?"

"Yes, brother." I left Luke's office, closing the door behind me. I had just gotten away with murder, and yet I felt less safe than I ever had. I needed to get upstairs and talk to Mila immediately.

First to make sure she was okay after that confrontation, and second to tell her about my plan.

The timeline would need to be moved up with the Choosing so close, but I was certain we could still make it work. I crossed the room, deep in my thoughts.

Tybalt's voice startled me. "I found *this* at our front door." Tybalt had taken over door duty for Dogberry, and he came into the common room just as my foot hit the stairs. A small figure stood next to him. Probably another girl desperate for a roof over her head, poor thing. Except when she pushed her hood back, I froze.

"Avery?" I asked. I couldn't believe it. She knew better. How many lessons about safety had I drilled into her head?

Tybalt smiled up at me. "You know her?"

I turned and stomped across the room, wrenching Avery's arm out of Tybalt's grip. "What are you doing here?" I hissed, pulling her into the corner. A few of the brothers had entered the common room and were watching with interest. "How did you even know where I was?"

Avery rolled her eyes, snatching her arm out of my grasp. "I told you I knew what you did. And anyone with half a brain knows where the Kingsnakes operate. Besides, that's not important right now."

"Hey, Prospero," one of the brothers called over to me. "Who's the fine little piece you're hiding in the corner? She looking for a place to stay?"

I whipped my head around, glaring at the handful of men nearby. "She's not available. Mind your own business."

Another brother whistled. "Damn. Prospero's protective over this one." I gritted my teeth, closing my eyes. I wouldn't kill them. Not tonight.

"Avery, you need to tell me what's wrong and then you need to go. And where the hell is Ella?"

The men murmured among themselves. "Oh shit, guys. She kinda looks like Prospero. Think this could be his sister?"

In my head, I was plotting their eventual murder, dragging it out. Even Avery looked stunned at the fury in my eyes.

"Avery?" I prompted.

"If it is his sister, he can't call dibs on her. Even in the apocalypse that shit's wrong." I cranked my neck around, offering a death stare to the men in the corner. All they did was smile back. Avery better have a damn good reason for coming here, because she just put all of us in danger. "Avery. Problem," I ground out. "What is it?"

"Ella," she whispered. "Ella is sick. I left her in the apartment with Mrs. Mullins. But you need to come home. I think she needs a doctor."

I was certain my heart stopped beating. Ever since Ella caught the sickness after my mom, her health hadn't been great. It was only a matter of time before she got sick again, but not tonight. Please, God, not tonight. Not with Mila hiding upstairs, and Luke waiting for me to slip up. But I couldn't leave Ella home sick. I nodded, pushing Avery toward the door.

"Wait for me outside." She didn't have to be told twice, darting through the doorway without another word. Avery gone, I turned back to the men still in the room. "Tell Brother Brutus I had to go home for a family emergency. And if one of you even glances at my female, or my sister, again... I will have no problem making you disappear."

I eyed each man individually, scanning them for fear or weakness. "Am I fucking clear?" One nodded, and the rest just stared blankly back. Sheep, doing as they were told.

The sooner I could get us all out of here, the better. I hoped Mila would understand when I didn't come up to her room. I'd explain when I got the chance. I turned and followed Avery out into the night. She stood just outside the door, huddled in her sweater. "What the hell were you thinking coming out here?" She glared at me, her gray eyes pissed in the moonlight.

"I didn't have a choice, Ray. Ella's fever is really bad. It was either I came and found you, or you came home and found her." I sighed, pushing my hood back and running my hand through my hair. "Is she that bad?"

"It's not good. She was fine one minute, and the next she was burning up." Avery bounced from leg to leg. I was pissed at her for endangering herself, but deep down I knew she wouldn't have come here unless there was no other choice.

"All right. Let's go." I took off at a brisk pace through the streets, Avery tagging close behind. I turned to glare at her in the faint moonlight. "Promise me you'll never come back here."

"I promise." She stuck her tongue out. "No offense, but that place was friggin' creepy."

"Language."

"Yeah, yeah."

We were quiet as we walked the blocks back to the apartment. It wasn't far, thankfully. "What did you tell Mrs. Mullins?" I asked.

"I told her you were at the bar with some friends," she murmured. Smart girl. The bar was one place men still hung out, despite all the problems with the world. I personally didn't go, but Mrs. Mullins wouldn't question it.

I shook my head. "Still. I can't believe she let you go to the bar by yourself at night."

We rounded the corner to our apartment, and Avery paused at the bottom of the fire escape. "What choice did she have, Ray? What choice do any of us have?"

God, she was too damn young to be so wise. She deserved to have a real childhood, a chance at youth. Not this. I followed her up the ladder to our floor, where Mrs. Mullins was pacing our living room. Ella was tossing and turning on the couch. "Nice of you to show up," my neighbor snapped at me. "Just like a man to be out drinking and avoiding his responsibilities."

I wanted to snap back, and tell her exactly what I was doing, but that would only lead to more problems. So I kept my mouth shut, and smiled at the old woman. "I appreciate you staying with Ella. It's late, and I'm sure you want to get home. Thanks again."

I quickly ushered Mrs. Mullins back to the fire escape, with her muttering about disappointing young people the entire way. Some things never changed, even with the end of the world. I locked the windowdoor behind her, and turned back to Avery with a sigh. "Thank you for thinking enough to leave someone with your sister, but my God that woman drives me crazy." Avery flashed me a quick smile from next to the couch.

"Tell me about it. I got a ten minute lecture about not brushing my hair before I could leave." I joined Avery on the floor, pressing the back of my hand to Ella's forehead. Avery was right. She was burning up. Coughs and sniffles we could handle, no problem. But fevers... fevers could be dangerous. "We need to get her into the shower."

I picked Ella up into my arms, and raced over to the shower, praying there'd be enough water. She barely opened her eyes as I ran, mumbling incoherent words. She was still conscious, so that was a good sign. We couldn't afford the doctor to come out here in the middle of the night unless it was absolutely necessary. Medicine was hard to find, so we were going to have to break it the old- fashioned way, and hope for the best.

I didn't bother taking either of our clothes off as I turned on the tap full blast, sending up silent thanks when the cool water came rushing out of the shower head. I sat with Ella on the cracked floor of the shower, rocking her slender body like I did when she was a baby. I could hear Avery out in the kitchen, opening cupboards. She was a smart kid, and if anything happened to me, I knew she'd take care of Ella as best as she could. I don't know how long we sat in the shower. Long enough for the water to weaken from a steady stream to a weaker drizzle.

Goosebumps covered my arms, but when I pressed my hand to Ella's forehead, it was cooler than before. I shut the tap off, and carried her to her bedroom, stripping off her wet clothes and dressing her in the lightest nightgown I could find in her drawer.

Her fever breaking was a good sign, but we weren't over the worst of it yet. "Here." Avery came up behind me, carrying damp towels. "You get changed, and I'll handle this." I nodded.

"Thanks." I ran back into the bathroom, changing into dry clothes as quickly as I could. By the time I made it back to the girls' room, Avery was sitting on the bed next to Ella, brushing her hair. She had put a cool towel around each of her thighs, and around the back of her neck – just like we had done with our mom.

She looked up at me. "She doesn't seem as agitated. I think she's actually sleeping now." I put my hand to her cheek. Still warm, but definitely cooler than before. "If she's still hot in the morning, I'll get the doctor. Right now, all we can do is wait." I sat on the floor, resting my head against what used to be my bed.

I pressed my fingers to Ella's wrist every so often, making sure she didn't start getting warm again. Beside her, Avery was quiet for so long, I thought she had fallen asleep.

"Ray?" Avery whispered.

Guess not. "Yeah?"

"Did you meet a girl? At the motel, I mean. I know you're not supposed to, but..." she trailed off, embarrassed.

I wanted to laugh, but I couldn't. Because she was right. "Why do you think that?"

"You leave the house earlier, and come home later. And you don't seem to be as sad when you come home either. Sometimes you're even smiling. So I just hoped..."

I didn't respond right away. Would she even remember?

163

"It's Mila." The bed shifted with a creak as Avery sat up. "Mila, your college girlfriend you thought was dead, Mila?" This time I couldn't stop my laughter. "How do you even remember Mila?"

"I don't, really. But I heard you and mom talking about her." Avery was quiet, but I could practically hear her gears turning.

"Spit it out."

"Do you still love her?"

I took a deep breath in. "It's not that simple anymore, Avery. Love isn't just love." Of course I still loved her. How could I not? Mila was my flickering of light in the growing darkness. She was a drug I don't think I had ever gotten over. But divulging this to my little sister just seemed weird.

"You should tell her you love her." I wanted to scold her, but hearing her sound so hopeful about something made my heart swell.

I smiled to myself. "You're impossible, you know that? I'll tell you what, if we make it to the morning in one piece, I'll tell Mila I love her."

"Promise?" she whispered.

"I promise."

We sat like that until dawn, quietly sitting in our own feelings and thoughts. Avery and I took turns wetting the towels, making sure they stayed cool for Ella. Just before the sun broke through the night, Ella turned over in bed.

"Ray?" she asked sleepily. "What are you doing in my bedroom?" I wanted to swing her round the room and kiss her forehead until she screamed for me to stop.

Instead I just rose to my knees and gave her a smile. "Just checking in on one of my two favorite girls."

She smiled back before closing her eyes and drifting back into an easy sleep. Avery met my gaze over Ella's sleeping body. "Go. I've got this. And you've got a promise to keep."

One way or another, these women were going to be the death of me.

FIFTEEN
Mila

I tossed and turned in my bed, unable to get comfortable. I had assumed Ray would follow me upstairs almost immediately, but as dusk fell into full night, I realized he wasn't coming. Where was he? Was he safe? Alive?

Nothing was ever a certainty after the Collapse. Surely I understood that concept better than most.

Eventually I turned my lamp off, pretending like I was going to sleep. I couldn't exactly go downstairs and check to make sure he was okay, especially after the close call with Laura and Brother Brutus. Sometimes I really hated this world. I hadn't realized how simple life was before. Worried about your boyfriend? You texted him, or called him.

Now, you lay in bed and imagined thousands of horrific scenarios, all ending with his body at the bottom of a ditch.

I stared up at my ceiling, barely lit by the waning moon. Some of the popcorn texture was scraped away, and I wondered who had been bored enough to pick at the layers of plaster. Bored, or desperate. You would've had to stand on the bed frame to reach it, so I was going to go with desperate.

Eventually the night bled into the purple bruise of dawn, and I managed to close my eyes for a moment or two.

When I opened them again, the orange tone of the morning sun was painting over night. Someone knocked lightly at my door. I narrowed my eyes at the noise, wondering who was disturbing the sleep I had just managed to fall into, when Ray poked his head in. He was maskless, but still wore the black hoodie of the Kingsnakes.

"Ray," I breathed. All of last night's anxiety fell away, seeing his face look just as tired as mine. "What the hell happened to you?" Ray did a double take behind his back, then slid into my room. He closed the door silently and came to sit at the head of my small mattress with me. "I was on my way upstairs, when Avery showed up at the door."

Avery? Here? "What the hell was she thinking?" I sat up, crossing my legs, and looked Ray in the eyes. "How did she even know where to find you?" I still couldn't picture the tiny toddler I had pushed on the swings as an almost-teenager, grown and with a mind of her own. It just didn't compute.

He sighed. "Those were basically my exact words. But Avery isn't stupid. She knows what I do, and where to find me. Ella was sick last night. Really sick. We were up all night trying to keep her fever down." I looked more closely at him, at the dark circles ringing his eyes.

Ray wasn't lying when he said he'd been up all night – just like me. "Shit, I'm sorry. Is she okay?" Ray nodded, giving me a crooked smile.

"She's through the worst of it. The fever broke just before dawn." He was quiet for a moment, his eyes unfocused. "I don't think it helps being in that apartment building. Everyone is living on top of one another, and her immune system is still weak from whatever she caught after mom died."

"So then why are you here? Ella still needs you. And if anyone catches you here in the morning, especially after last night..." I didn't even want to think about the consequences.

"I'm here because of a promise I made." He laughed quietly and pulled me into his chest. I rested against him and watched his gray eyes. "And because I have a plan to get us out of here."

"You do?" My eyes widened. We had been planning an escape for a while, but nothing seemed feasible, especially with two young girls. But this time, Ray seemed fairly certain. "How?"

"We're going to use the dramatics of the Choosing to sneak away. I'm on door duty with Dogberry that day, so we don't need to worry about another brother watching the front door. Besides, I got first choice last month, so I'll be one of the last to choose this month. If we sneak out in the morning or early afternoon, we should have hours before anyone realizes either of us is missing. Ella is still weak, but she's light enough we can carry her if need be. I'll pack as many extra supplies for her as I can."

The brothers on door duty had been one of the biggest obstacles in our getaway plan. We could take down one, but not the other before the brothers who stayed with the pregnant girls would realize something was going on. Ray being on door duty would be a huge help.

"Ella and Avery?" I asked.

"There's a shed around the back of the motel. No one uses it. I've hidden the supplies in there, in a couple backpacks, and I'll sneak the girls in there in the morning. The plan is to get as far away from the motel as possible." He chewed on his lip, and I knew what was coming next.

"Don't start that again, Ray." He glared down at me.

"I need to know my sisters are safe if I have to stay behind."

I sighed. "Of course they'll be safe. But if we're leaving, we're leaving together." It was my turn to think for a moment. "What about the rest of the girls? We can't just leave them here."

"Some of them will want to stay, babydoll. It's the only safety they've ever known." Ray ran his fingers through my hair, stroking my cheeks. "But we'll leave the door unlocked behind us for those who want to leave. Like Hannah."

Hannah. I pressed my lips together and nodded. "Hannah deserves another chance. I'll let her know to be ready."

Ray pulled me tighter to his chest. "Hannah you can tell. But no one else. She can let the other girls know after we're far enough away. I can't take any chances with your or my sisters' safety."

"I know. I know." I burrowed deeper into him, letting his heartbeat lull me into a false sense of security.

"Was that the promise you mentioned?"

"Hmm?" he asked absentmindedly. His fingers were trailing up and down my back.

"You said you were here this early because you had a promise to keep. Was the promise telling me about the escape plan?"

Ray laughed, his chest vibrating under my ear. "Unfortunately not." He pulled me up and over, so I sat on his lap with a leg on either side. "The promise in question is one I made my incredibly precocious and determined little sister."

I rolled my eyes. "Sounds like someone else I know."

"Shush." He smiled at me, but his gray eyes looked nervous.

"You're a member of an illicit underground breeding ring. Whatever you have to tell me, it can't be worse than that."

Ray cocked his head to the side. "Depends on what you mean by worse." He put a hand on either of my cheeks, watching me carefully. "I love you, Mila."

I was silent, unable to speak with so many emotions twisting inside me.

"I loved you the first moment I laid eyes on you. I loved you the day you left, and I thought you had run away from me." He took a deep breath, not looking away. "I loved you every day you were gone, even the days I was certain you were dead. I loved you the day I saw you on your knees downstairs, and every day since. Mila, there is no one else for me in the entire world. I can survive the apocalypse, but I can't survive a life without *you*."

How was I supposed to respond to such a confession? I opened my mouth and closed it what felt like a thousand times.

"Goddammit, Mila, say something." Ray gripped my cheeks tighter, his eyes blazing with a passion I hadn't seen in a long time. "Even telling me to fuck off would be better than this silence."

"Ray, I love you too. I always have. Always will." I sighed, trying to look away from him, but he held my face still. "Love is quite possibly the stupidest thing in the world right now, but there it is. I love you."

He shook his head and smiled. "No, babydoll. Love is the only thing that keeps us sane."

I leant forward, pressing my lips against his. "I love you. I love you so damn much." And then I tangled my fingers in his curls, kissing him like I had never kissed anyone before.

Ray moaned into my mouth, his tongue darting in and out. "You are the sweetest fucking thing I've ever tasted."

I sighed. Nothing felt better than Ray's lips, kissing me, moving down my neck. His touch sent shivers across my body, and he smiled against my collarbone.

"If I remember correctly, you taste this good everywhere." He pulled my shirt up and I helped him tug it the rest of the way off. "Fuck," I muttered as his head immediately bent down again to pull one of my nipples into his mouth. One of his hands found my other nipple, twisting it just enough to walk the line between pain and pleasure. His other hand held me in place, digging into my skin as if he was afraid I would disappear. "Ray, God."

171

He sat up and grinned, tugging his hoodie and shirt over his head and tossing them to the end of the bed. "Only one of us can be in bed with you right now, babydoll. Choose wisely."

"Get back over here and finish what you started." I wasn't sure if it was a demand or a plea. I just needed to feel Ray everywhere.

Luckily, Ray didn't need to be asked twice. He moved back over me, unzipping my pants and pulling them down. They, along with my panties, joined the pile of clothes at the bottom of my bed. Then he settled between my legs, his tongue testing the wetness I knew he would find there. I arched my back, pleasure racing through my veins. "Told you," he whispered. "Best thing I've tasted in years."

I didn't pay attention to his words anymore, lost to the sensation of his tongue exploring and licking, making me feel things I had thought weren't possible any longer. I cursed when his mouth covered my aching clit and sucked lightly.

"Mmm..." Ray stopped for a moment, looking up at me. "Do you like that? Knowing how crazy the taste of you makes me? Knowing that nothing else will ever compare to *this*?" He bent his head back over me, plunging his tongue deep into my pussy.

"Jesus," I cried. Ray moved his tongue up to my clit, swirling it around until I was sure I would combust. Then he stopped again, pulling his mouth away, leaving my body trembling on the edge of release. A finger slipped inside me, barely easing the craving I had for *more*.

172

"Come on my tongue, babydoll. Let me taste everything you have. I'll give you what we both need."

I moaned, clutching the bedsheets in my hands. I didn't care how, but he needed to make me come before I went crazy. "Ray, please."

A second finger joined the first, and he bit down lightly on my clit. That was all it took for my body to give in to its release, Ray stroking his fingers and licking me through my orgasm. "Just like that. Fuck, you're beautiful."

I rested my head back on my thin pillow, waiting for my vision to return to normal. "Remind me why I hid in a forest for ten years."

Ray laughed. "All I know is we have a lot of lost time to make up for."

I couldn't see him from my position, but I could hear him unzipping his pants. The thick head of his cock nudged into me, teasing my still-pulsing pussy. I was so sensitive, I was sure I would come again as he slowly eased himself inside. Every nerve felt alive, desperate for more of whatever Ray could give.

"Mila," Ray whispered in a strangled voice. "You're so goddamn tight." He pulled back, letting me savor every sweet inch of his cock. I wasn't sure how I had survived on my own for so long. How could I have lived without *this*?

But it took too many words to explain, and my voice was stolen by Ray pushing himself back inside me. "I love you so fucking much," he muttered. There was a tenderness to his movements, a slowness as he withdrew and sank deep inside once more, and it was driving me to the brink again.

"I'll follow you wherever you go, you know that?"

"I know," I breathed. My voice cut off with a moan as his cock pushed even deeper. His movements quickened, tenderness transforming into desperation. "You're never leaving me again."

"No," I whispered. I grabbed for the bedsheets again, looking for some purchase to anchor me through Ray's thrusts. Raising my hips, I met him each time he plunged back into me. My breaths turned into gasps, my body ready to cave to his demands once more.

"Come for me, Mila. Come for me and only me. Only ever me." He drove himself harder, faster, grinding against my clit. It was too much, too many different sensations, and I couldn't control my need to let go.

We came at the same time, his name a sigh on my lips as pleasure rushed through my veins and spread throughout my limbs. Ray whispered my name as he released and trembled inside me.

God. I never wanted to be alone ever again. I never wanted to be without Ray ever again. He grimaced when he withdrew, lying next to me on the bed and pulling me to lie on top. I absentmindedly traced the rough snake tattooed on his chest, until he stilled my hand.

"Once you're in, you're in for life," he murmured. "It's why I haven't tried to leave before now. Because they would always come looking, and where would I hide with two young girls?" There was a hesitation in his voice, as if he was afraid of what my response would be. But we had all done things to get by in this world.

We all had marks on our souls, stains on our hearts. Ray's just happened to be visible, tattooed on his skin for all to see. "What changed your mind?" He squeezed me close.

"Some girl I used to know showed up. She reminded me what it was like to have hope. Or was just stubborn enough to make an escape work."

I laughed quietly. The second option sounded more likely. Regardless, I was happy Ray had decided to take the chance. Even if we died trying...

No. I couldn't afford to think like that. We'd all get out of here, alive. Safe. Free. That was the only option I allowed to take up space in my mind. I rested my head on Ray's chest, listening to the steady beats of his heart and the quiet breaths he drew. This was what had been missing from my life in the woods. Ray. Love. People. Maybe I had made a mistake in staying isolated for so long. Maybe I should've tried harder to find him on my supply runs. Or maybe that would've been a big mistake too. He ran his hands over my bare skin, and as our breaths slowed, we drifted off into an easy rest together.

A quiet knock at my door startled us both from our dozing. "Ray," I hissed. "Ray, hide!" He gave me a look of bewilderment, still half asleep, when he darted underneath the thin blankets. It wouldn't do much at all to hide him, but hopefully I'd be able to stall whoever was in the hallway.

"One second!" I pulled on my clothes, positive I looked a hot mess, and stumbled to see who it was. It had to be another girl, because no brother would wait so long to be granted entrance.

I swung open the door to find an exhausted-looking Hannah on the other side.

"Hey," she murmured. "Can I come in?"

"Umm..." I looked over my shoulder to see a very clear human-sized lump on my bed. "Now isn't really a great time." Hannah rolled her eyes.

"Yeah, you got better plans? Come on, it's important." It must have been important because she pushed past me into my room. She left the door open just a sliver – approved by the Kingsnakes. I couldn't breathe. Hopefully, Ray could stay hidden. Or if she noticed, hopefully she could keep our secret. I hadn't told her because I was hoping to keep her safe. If she knew, she'd become an accomplice.

"What's up?" I asked. She looked even worse than yesterday, dark circles ringing both eyes, and her pallor was whiter than paper.

"Well... uh..." She twisted her hands inside the sleeves of her worn sweater, not meeting my eyes. "Maybe I should sit down." Before I could protest, Hannah sat on the end of my bed, right on top of Ray's leg. My eyes widened, and she looked at me in confusion.

"Mila... is there someone in your bed?" I couldn't tell if there was shock or teasing lacing her voice.

"Um, well you see, I was just trying to protect you. I didn't want you to have to hide another secret, and uh..." I trailed off as she whipped the covers off my bed, exposing a shirtless Ray. Thank God, he grabbed the sheet before she saw anything else. "Holy shit," she whispered. "So there *was* some truth to Laura's accusations after all."

Ray smiled awkwardly. "It's kind of a long story." Hannah shook her head, looking back and forth between us. "I don't even know where to start. But if you guys are happy, then I'm happy. As messed up as all of this is."

I breathed a silent prayer. I knew if she wasn't half as distracted, it would've been a hell of a lot longer conversation. I'd take what I could get.

I chewed on my lip, and Ray silently motioned to get Hannah out of the room. I knew he needed to leave as soon as he could, but Hannah was lost in a world of her own, staring through the open slats of my window. "Uh, Hannah? You said it was important?"

"Oh, yeah." She tossed her red hair out of her face, giving me a sad smile. "It just felt wrong to ruin the first moment of happiness any of us have experienced with what I have to tell you."

Ray and I met each other's eyes. There was no way to know what she was going to say. Has the Choosing been moved up? Any number of things could go wrong to screw up our plans. "Okay..."

Hannah took a deep breath and threw her shoulders back. "I'm pregnant."

SIXTEEN

12 YEARS AGO

Ray

As soon as I stepped out of my air-conditioned car, I regretted my choice of clothes. It was too damn hot – even in September – for jeans. I was trying to make a good first impression, with it being my first day on campus, but man. Fuck these jeans. I was going to melt before I even made it to my first lecture.

You'll never survive without me.

I really shouldn't have been surprised. Changing seasons were nothing but a memory, long past. But I had gotten used to cooler temperatures further north, at my old university. Snatching my backpack from the backseat, I sighed and looked up at the sprawling campus. In theory, it shouldn't be difficult to find my English class, located in the elegantly named Hayes Hall. In theory.

The parking lot was nearly empty, only a few cars filling the massive space. Gas was expensive, and most families shared cars – if they could afford one at all.

I was planning on selling my car soon too, now a luxury I didn't need, but I just hadn't gotten around to it yet.

August had been a chaotic mess of swapping credits and classes, and finding housing that wouldn't break the bank. The university I had been attending was four hours away, which didn't seem that bad as a high school senior.

But now, with how quickly the world was changing, I needed to be closer to home, since my mom and stepdad were expecting a baby. Family was the most important thing in life, and Mom needed help. I withdrew from my courses, transferring to the university that ate up a large portion of my home city. Being only halfway through my degree had made it easy to switch.

To be honest, I really didn't see the point of university anymore. We all attended lectures and seminars, doing our group projects and our essays like there was something to look forward to once we earned our degrees.

In reality, trades jobs were a lot more stable these days, and a university degree didn't mean you wouldn't end up stocking the local grocery store for minimum wage anyway. A pretty piece of paper was all it really was.

But people still tried to maintain normalcy, despite the rising temperatures, and schools still pushed university, so seniors kept applying. If I didn't have a full ride scholarship, I probably would've left a long time ago.

I had a full-time job waiting for me at the grain mill I had worked at since I was a teen, but Mom wanted me to "follow my dreams," whatever that meant anymore.

I found my way inside the first imposing gray building. Students pushed past me, hurrying to their next class. I hoped I was in the right building. It looked like the right one from the map I had studied this morning.

"Excuse me." A tall girl squeezed past me, rushing with a half-zipped backpack. I wanted to point it out to her, but I stopped myself. These days people didn't talk to people they didn't know. They were scared of the unknown. Not that I could blame them. But I was more afraid of what I did know. Mainly that I couldn't find my damn class.

"You're blocking everybody, man." A guy wearing gym shorts shouldered me, and I realized I had been standing still in the middle of the hall.

Fuck. Now I was definitely going to be late. I glanced up at the clock on the sterile white wall. I had three minutes to find my lecture hall. Apparently the buffer I had given myself wasn't enough. And to make matters worse, my T-shirt was drenched in sweat.

Unfortunately for me, the university wasn't air conditioned either. No wonder so many of the students dressed in shorts and dresses.

I jogged up to what I hoped was a professor, wearing a badge and standing outside an open door. "I'm looking for room H1022. This is Hayes Hall, right?"

The man gave me a look of sympathy over his glasses, shaking his head.

"This is the McKinley Centre. Hayes Hall is the building to the left if you go back out the doors. There's a big eagle statue out front. It's not far, but you'll want to hurry."

The clock with its giant analog numbers glared back at me, taunting me with every second I had wasted. "Thanks."

He called something after me, but I was already racing through the now-empty hall. The heat didn't faze me as much as it did the first time, the university buildings were just as hot inside as out. Fucking global warming. Wasn't it supposed to make everything colder?

I turned left, and immediately saw the giant eagle. By the time I opened the door, the hallway was completely empty. Because I was now officially late to my first class on my first day. Fan-fucking-tastic. Thankfully, H1022 wasn't too far from the front.

I took a moment outside the double doors to compose my breathing. My only hope was that the class was incredibly full, and one person sneaking in a minute or two late wouldn't be noticeable. I opened the door as slowly as I could, grimacing at the creak as it swung open.

H1022 was a massive lecture hall, the semi-circle kind with staggered seating around a stage for the professor. And this massive lecture hall was filled with exactly one professor, looking at me in irritation from his pulpit, and ten students.

"I'm going to assume you are..." The professor looked at his notes, running his finger down what had to be a very short list. "Mr. Ray Dawson. I didn't think I was going to have to deal with tardiness in a third-year course."

I took a couple of steps down, hoping to slide into a desk near the top and be done entirely with this embarrassing situation. Was it too late to transfer back to my old school? "Uhh... yes, I apologize for my lateness. I just transferred here, and got a little mixed up with the buildings."

I could already tell this professor was one of the ones clinging too hard to the past. A past where English professors were admired and honored. Now people looked at them and wondered how they fed their families. He openly rolled his eyes at me, and waved his hand. "I'll let it pass this time. Just take a seat, and we can continue discussing the syllabus."

I slid into the closest seat, five or six rows above the next student. The professor cleared his throat. "A little bit closer if you please, Mr. Dawson. No point in me straining my voice if I don't have to."

Dick. I got back out of my seat, certain every student was staring at my sweaty shirt. I peeked up as I stepped down, checking out the next safest row, and grabbed a desk next to a dark-haired girl. I sighed, leaning back in my chair as the professor droned on about course expectations and exams. I needed to talk to my mom about this. I know she wanted me to do "normal" things, but surely I'd be of better use bringing in an income. As I dragged out my notebook and a pen, a scrap of paper slid across my desk. Out of the corner of my eye, I looked at the girl next to me, but her eyes were focused on the professor.

She was cute, from what I could see. Long, dark hair, and bare shoulders freckled by the summer sun. And apparently we were passing notes.

Don't worry about Professor Lewis. He's a dick.

I smiled for the first time that morning, and scribbled a quick note back.

Maybe it's the lack of A/C?

She snorted quietly. I was no longer paying attention to anything Professor Dick said. Writing notes with a potentially cute girl next to me was the most excitement I'd had in weeks.

The scrap of paper slid back across my desk.

A/C went down last year. Keeping the football team active was more important to the board than making sure we all don't sweat to death. At the bottom of her note was a tiny drawing of an eagle carrying a football – the same eagle outside the hall – with a banner that read "SOS."

I held back a laugh, not wanting to irritate the professor further. *Remind me to wear shorts tomorrow.*

Her response was nearly immediate.

Remind me to fake a devastating illness tomorrow.

I drummed my pen on my desk, already captivated by this girl. I wanted to see her face. What did she look like? What color were her eyes? Did her smile match her sense of humor? She probably had the best laugh.

But then who will keep me company in class?

I held my breath. Maybe I'd crossed the line with a girl who didn't even know my name. People liked their safety, after all. Their privacy. But the scrap of paper was already back on my desk.

You're right. You'll never survive without me.

Next to it, she'd drawn a small Tic-Tac-Toe board, with the first X already marked. I smiled to myself, scrawled my O, and sent it back. Professor Lewis droned on, and I played Tic-Tac-Toe with the nameless girl. He passed out yellowing books, and we moved on to Hangman.

He started reading passages from an ancient book of Shakespeare, even though it had little relevance to our lives. They should've been teaching us how to grow vegetables out of nothing, and how to stitch up a loose hem. Instead, Professor Lewis read Shakespeare, and we moved back to Tic-Tac-Toe.

Finally, the professor looked up at the clock. "All right, that's it for today. Read pages 1 to 50 for homework, and be prepared to discuss them tomorrow."

I stuffed my notebook into my backpack, suddenly equal parts nervous and excited to see the mystery girl's face. I tried to imagine it to no avail. Had she tried to picture mine? "Mr. Dawson!"

Professor Lewis's voice cut through my thoughts. "Yes, professor?" He looked at me with a frown. There was a blotch of ketchup on his tie, and I wanted to point it out to him, but somehow I didn't think that would help my situation. "I expect you to be on time tomorrow."

"Yes, sir." He turned away from me to talk to a brown-noser next to him, and I knew this was it. This was the moment I would turn and see her face. Why was I so nervous? All we had done was pass notes and play games like we were in grade school again. I turned in my seat, ready to thank my mystery girl for keeping me sane through class.

Instead, I found myself speechless. In front of me sat the most beautiful woman I had ever seen. Her white tank top only emphasized her tanned skin, covering taut muscles.

Dark waves framed a face free of makeup – not that she needed it. Surely I was imagining things. How could I get along with someone so well, passing notes and playing games, and she was this stunning? The heat must be getting to me. My mystery girl smirked. "Hi."

"Hi." I wasn't sure how I managed to get the syllable out of my mouth. She probably thought I was a doofus, taking pity on the idiot sitting next to her.

"You're pretty bad at Tic-Tac-Toe. It's a good thing it won't be on the final exam, otherwise you'd be screwed." Her green eyes twinkled with mischief, and I laughed out loud.

"It's okay, because you're terrible at Hangman. Who waits until the last second to guess vowels?"

"Maybe I was just giving you a chance to win at something." By now, students for the next class were trickling in, but I didn't want to stop talking. I wanted to hear her laugh first. Hell, I wanted to *make* her laugh.

I chewed on the inside of my cheek to stop myself from smiling like a fool. "Keep telling yourself that. We have all semester to see who the real Hangman champion is."

She shook her dark hair back over her shoulders, a loud laugh escaping her mouth and echoing in the still-quiet room. It was everything I had imagined it would be, and I wanted to bottle it up so I could experience it every single day. This girl was special. I couldn't mess this up.

Your name idiot – tell her your name!

185

I grinned at her, so enamored by her natural beauty and the easy way her laugh made her come alive. She was water, flowing whichever way the brook took her, and I found myself yearning to float along with her.

"I'm Ray." I stuck out my hand. She smiled back, one of her bottom teeth slightly crooked. On anyone else, it would've stood out – a stain on a canvas. On her, it only added to her allure. She grasped my hand firmly.

"Mila. I was planning on meeting a friend for lunch, but you're welcome to come along if you'd like."

"Your friend won't mind?" As much as I wanted to know more about Mila, I didn't want to be the awkward third wheel if the "friend" ended up being her boyfriend.

Mila shook her head. "Not at all. She's my roommate, so I'm sure she's sick of me by now anyways."

I grabbed my backpack and followed Mila out the double doors. The heat of the day and the discomfort of my jeans were long forgotten. Had I gotten lost on my way to class? I couldn't remember. All I knew was this dark-haired girl in front of me was everything I had ever wanted in life, and I would follow her to the ends of the earth.

SEVENTEEN

Mila

*H*oly *fuck*. I hadn't been expecting those words to come out of Hannah's mouth. From the look on Ray's face, neither was he. The brothers did their best to make sure we got pregnant, but there were still ways for the girls to try and avoid it. We were women, after all.

Adaptable, if nothing else. Most of them were dangerous, but the idea of bringing a child into this world was scarier for a lot of them. Hannah pressed her lips together, her eyes fearful. "Hannah, how the hell did this happen?" I crossed the few steps to my bed, sitting next to her and wrapping my arms around her thin shoulders.

She sucked in a shaky breath. "I have no idea. I was being so careful, every time after he left. So fucking careful..." Her words trailed off as she broke into a silent sob.

"I even fucking prayed. I should've known none of those old wives' tales would work. It was stupid to be so hopeful."

A baby used to be something to be celebrated. Cherished. Now it only meant another mouth to feed, and another innocent life to protect. And here, in the motel, it meant pain and heartbreak as well. The pregnant girls were hidden away from the rest of us in a separate wing of the motel.

The East Wing. I'd heard some of the other girls whisper that they were watched day and night, leaving them with the bare minimum so they didn't try to abort the babies – or worse. The Kingsnakes didn't take any chances with their precious commodities.

I squeezed Hannah's shaking body, rubbing her arms. "Hey. It's gonna be okay. We're going to figure this out." The bed shifted behind me, and I glanced back to watch Ray shimmy into his pants and pull his shirt on before getting out of bed.

Hannah looked up at me, her pale face streaked with tears. "You can't know that, Mila. I can only hide it from them for so long. And then they'll trap me with those other girls, and I'll either die giving birth or they'll take my baby away from me and sell him like he's a loaf of bread."

"Do you..." I didn't know how to ask the question. But I knew I needed to support her either way, and figure out a way to help her before the brothers found out. "Do you want to keep the baby?"

"I don't want him to be sold. But I don't see what other choice I have. They're going to find out eventually." She buried her face in her hands again, crying softly.

I met Ray's gaze with a helpless look, watching him as he paced the worn wooden floor. "We're not going to let that happen, Hannah," he announced. "They're not going to lay a finger on you or your baby."

I nodded, my jaw tightening. "Ray's right."

She peeked her eyes out through her hands. "How?" For the first time since I had met Hannah, her eyes glimmered with the slightest bit of hope.

I turned to face her. "Ray has a plan for getting us out of here, during the Choosing. You just need to keep it together until then, okay? One more night. Can you do that for me?" I reached out and squeezed her hands.

Hannah stared at Ray, a question in her eyes. "A plan that will actually work?" Ray paused his pacing, looking at both of us. "I wouldn't risk my sisters' lives unless I was sure it was going to work." Ray briefly ran through the plan for Hannah, explaining how he was on door duty tomorrow, and would take out the other guard.

"If everything goes to plan, Mila will be able to grab you before the rest of the girls meet for lunch. Both of you will head down the stairs as quickly as possible, and meet my sisters in the shed." I turned back to Hannah. She seemed to have calmed down quite a bit with Ray's explanation. "You're welcome to come with us. I don't know where we'll end up, but it'll be far away from here."

"Thank you, but I think I need to go home. Especially with someone else relying on me now." She rubbed her belly, staring down at it like she couldn't quite believe what was happening inside her.

"But trust me when I say that's the last time I go to the grocery store on my own."

I would've laughed, had it not been for the absurd situation we were all living in. But, a thought occurred to me. "Wait. Hannah was going to tell the rest of the girls the doors were unlocked. Who will do that now?"

Hannah perked her head up. "I can still tell Stacy to meet me at my room sometime before the Choosing, but after we've left. I obviously won't be there, but I'll leave a note for her. She'll get the other girls out."

"Good thinking." I knew Stacy as an acquaintance only. But I knew she would be one of the most reliable ones to get the girls out safely. "Are we good then? Ready?"

"As ready as we'll ever be." Ray sighed, stuffing his hands in his pockets. "I'm sorry, Hannah. I'm so sorry this happened to you. Nothing in this life is fucking fair anymore."

Hannah ran her hand through her hair. "Don't be sorry. You did the best you could. Besides, maybe everything happened for a reason. I don't think I'd be as quick to jump on your escape scheme if I wasn't pregnant." She wrapped her arms around her belly. "I am *not* letting this baby be sold. He deserves to know love."

I looked up at Ray, and he smiled back at me. "I think we all do," he murmured.

Hannah rose to her feet. "I should head back to my room. And you should get going before your ass ends up caught." She pointed at Ray. "I can't believe neither of you told me about this. I can't believe Laura was right."

"Shush." I laughed, walking with her to the door. "Keep it together for one more day, okay? One more day, until we're getting the hell out of here. Be ready for our normal lunch time. We normally eat earlier anyways, so if anything goes wrong, it won't seem suspicious."

She gave me a tight hug. "Thank you," she whispered. And then she was gone, slipping back into the hallway.

I leaned against the closed door, shaking my head at Ray. "Is it safe? For her to go home?"

"Her parents live on the outskirts of the city, on a small farm. Hannah's a smart girl, Mila. She'll make it home no problem, and she definitely won't let herself get caught again." He walked over to me, resting his forehead against mine. "Besides, it's probably safer than trying to have a baby in the wild."

"You got me there."

"But..."

I raised my eyebrow at him. "But?"

Ray pressed his hand against my stomach, where our baby would grow if we ever had one. "Do you ever wonder what it would be like?"

"Of course I've wondered." I dreamed about it, the first few years after I left. The life I had given up for my supposed freedom. Wondering what our babies would look like, what Ray would be like as a father. All of it seemed far-fetched at this point. "But I think we should just try and survive for now."

Ray laughed. "Fair enough." He pressed a light kiss to my lips. "I should go."

"You should," I agreed. But neither of us moved, enjoying the quiet for just a moment longer. The next time he came back, it wouldn't be this peaceful. We would be stressed, trying to make sure we were able to slip away quietly. It would be hectic and overwhelming, and this second of peace felt important for everything that would follow.

"Okay," he groaned. "I'm going. I'll see you tomorrow. Be ready, okay? Bring only what you need."

I nodded. "I'll be waiting."

With one last kiss, he opened the door and snuck into the still-empty hallway. I watched him go, remaining in the relative safety of my room. The hall was deserted, no one around to see Ray's strong back retreat down the stairs. One more day. We just had to get through one more day.

I stepped back to close the door, ready to pass the time however I could until Ray returned. But just before I did, I heard the unmistakable sound of another door latching closed. Someone else had seen Ray leaving my room, and I had no idea who it was.

For the rest of the day, I avoided the rest of the girls like the plague. I had no idea who had seen Ray leave, or if they had seen him leave my room specifically, but I couldn't take any chances.

I had stashed a couple of granola bars under my bed, so food wasn't a problem, and I had showered the day before.

I stood in the middle of my room, trying to focus on packing my meager belongings instead of the potential of us getting caught. It wasn't much, but it was something to take my mind off things. My lighter was still safe in my pocket. It didn't have a lot of juice left, but it'd be in case of emergencies.

My clothes were clean. I didn't have much else to get ready. The Kingsnakes had taken my bag when I first arrived, so God only knew what happened to it. I came here with nothing, but I was leaving with a couple granola bars. And Ray.

I eyed the bedding on my mattress. It was thin and worn, but it was fabric, and who knew what the forecast held in store. I could bundle the pillow into the comforter for one of the girls to carry.

It would be awkward, but not overly heavy, and I was certain we'd be grateful for it when night fell.

The late afternoon sun chased the daylight, until finally it was dusk. I flipped on my camping lantern and took a seat on my bed. I would take my lantern as well, and if I went down to the kitchen just before lunch tomorrow it would likely be empty. I could grab some more food.

Not all of it, because I wanted to leave some behind for the girls who took advantage of the unlocked doors, but enough to have just in case. I lay on my bed, unable to sleep. I was anxious about tomorrow, terrified about all the things that could go wrong. We had to leave after Dogberry arrived, so he wouldn't see us from a distance and alert anyone else.

But we also had to leave early enough to give us a head start before anyone noticed we were missing, so the window of opportunity was small. There was a small possibility the brothers from the maternity ward would catch us, but their windows faced the front of the building.

With all these scenarios swirling in my head, I barely slept at all. Instead, I thought up exit strategies and Plan Bs, enough that I felt prepared for anything the Kingsnakes could throw at us. I was getting the hell out of here, Ray and his sisters in tow, and leaving a trail in my wake for the rest of the girls to follow.

Fuck the Kingsnakes who thought they could keep me down, the men who thought they could use a woman like a piece of property. I'd show them all what it looked like to really survive after the Collapse. I drifted in and out of sleep, not rested enough to feel refreshed, but enough to escape.

Eventually the night gave way to dawn, a brittle sun exorcizing the mist as I watched through the cracks in my window. It was going to be a beautiful day. Brisk and cool, but sunny. The kind of day where people would be playing in parks and inviting friends over for dinner.

It would also be the perfect day for us to escape. I snacked on a granola bar, listening for the sounds of the girls going for breakfast. Then I waited for them to return. When I knew I would be the only one in the kitchen, I cracked open my door wider and tiptoed to the stairs.

We weren't going to leave until later, but I could still stock up from the kitchen. None of the doors creaked open, and I breathed a sigh of relief.

At the bottom of the stairs, my relief turned into annoyance. Instead of the morning door brother I was expecting, Dogberry sat at a table playing solitaire.

This was *not* what we needed. I hoped Ray was already on his way. We were losing precious time if not.

"Well if it isn't my new girl of the month." He greeted me with a smile that made me want to gag. "Are you excited for tonight? I promise we'll have a lot more fun than boring Prospero." I shrugged, faking nonchalance.

"I guess we'll see if you're all talk or not after the Choosing."

"Believe me. I'm not all talk." He glared at me, slapping a card down on one of the stacks. "What are you doing down here anyways? All the girls already came for breakfast."

"I wasn't hungry until now. Is that okay?" I rolled my eyes, toeing the line just enough so he wouldn't think anything was out of the ordinary, but not enough to piss him off.

Dogberry turned back to his card game. "Whatever. Just don't make a mess."

I left Dogberry in the common room and went into the kitchen, which was thankfully empty. The cupboard that held all the small snack foods was relatively full, so I began picking through to get some protein bars and jerky that would be easy to pack and travel with. Digging through the cupboard meant my back was to the door, and when a hand stroked my back, I had to bite back a scream.

Fucking Dogberry. I took a deep breath, ignoring the loud racing of my heart. I was going to have to take him out before Ray got here.

Hopefully it wouldn't throw off our plans too much. I whirled around, ready to defend myself, only to see Ray standing in front of me.

"Jesus, Ray, you scared the shit out of me." I clutched my chest, sure my heart was going to beat right out of my ribs. "You shouldn't sneak up on me like that."

"I'm sorry, I thought you saw me." He rubbed my shoulders. "Are you all packed?"

I nodded, holding up my handful of snacks. "Just came down for a few more food bits we could bring with us. If we swing by my old camp in the forest, we can grab the rest of my supplies too."

"Good thinking." He smiled, a genuine grin filled with excitement. "The girls are hidden in the shed, and all the supplies are ready. I just need to take care of Dogberry, and then we can go. It's a little bit earlier than we thought we were going to leave. Do you think Hannah will be ready?"

I frowned, ignoring his question. "You didn't see him out in the common room? He was just there a second ago when I came down."

"No. He's probably doing his walkaround. Gives us five minutes to take care of some last-minute business." Ray leaned over me, pushing my back against the hard edge of the countertop. "Some really important business."

"I do *not* think we have time for this." I laughed, already distracted by his gray, wanting eyes. Ray wouldn't take chances unless it was absolutely safe, so I knew he had to be feeling fairly comfortable with the current situation.

"Give me two minutes," he breathed. "Two minutes, babydoll. This might be the last chance I ever get to have you, and I'll never forgive myself if I don't take the opportunity."

"Don't talk like that." I narrowed my eyes, and he stroked his hand down my neck. "We're all getting out of here."

"Just in case, then. I have so much nervous energy. I need to do something with it." His hand dipped lower, trailing the outline of my collarbone beneath my shirt. "The girls are safe. I can't remember the last time someone ventured into that shed. Everything is in place. We have a moment to steal for ourselves."

I already knew I couldn't deny him, but I looked up and nodded my assent anyways. He turned me around, pushing me so my chest pressed against the cool countertops. My pants hit the floor, and I heard his do the same a moment later. "You weren't kidding about two minutes," I murmured.

Not that I minded. It was damn hot when Ray took control like this. I clenched my legs together to ease the ache between them.

"Shut up," he whispered, nudging my legs wider with his knee. "I already know you're mine, babydoll. This is just to get it out of our system. Hold tight."

I gripped the other side of the narrow island, just as Ray sank deeply inside me. "Fuck," I cursed. My body was already spiraling. "Some warning would've been nice."

"You got a warning," he muttered, gripping my hips tightly with either hand. "I told you to hold tight. Now I'm telling you to not let go."

197

With that cautionary sentence, Ray pulled himself back and then slammed deep inside of me once more. And again. And again. Until all I felt was Ray claiming me, thrusting deeper and deeper until there was nowhere left for him to go. Until I was begging for release, for him to let me shatter around his cock, and ride the waves of pleasure I knew were so close.

"Promise me we'll get out of here together. All of us." I needed to hear it, the same way I needed air, and the way I needed him to fuck me until nothing hurt anymore.

"I promise." He continued to rock his hips, thrusting inside me, and slipped his hand around my front so he could press on my clit. "Show me you're mine, babydoll. Kingsnakes or no, you've always been mine."

He promised. I clung to that, and my body toppled over the edge of ecstasy, crying out his name like I wasn't supposed to be quiet. I shook through my orgasm as Ray continued to drive deep into my pussy, until he too was trembling, whispering my name as he came.

Ray pulled out and I turned around to see him looking for a dish towel to clean himself off with. Then he turned to me, doing the same between my legs. "Well," I whispered. Ray was on his knees in front of me, a reflection of the first time I had seen him in the motel. "Guess it's a good thing we're leaving, because that was *not* quiet."

"Knock knock!" The sound of Dogberry's voice in the common room had us separating, both of us rolling our eyes. I pulled up my pants and straightened my shirt, and Ray did the same, making sure his mask was in place.

198

"Guess that's our cue. Are you ready?" he whispered. "I'll take care of Dogberry while you sneak up the stairs. Go the back way, past the laundry room."

I nodded. "Go do what you need to do, and I'll make sure Hannah is good to go." Ray grabbed either side of my cheeks, kissing me deeply. His kiss was filled with longing and regret, but above all else, the slightest taste of hope. A chance of something good. "I love you, Mila. No matter what."

"I know." I pushed him back. "Now go!"

He gave me a small smile and stepped out into the common room. I turned to go out the back exit like he had instructed, but before I took a step Ray's snarl filled the kitchen and I knew something was horribly wrong.

"What the actual hell?" he growled.

Dogberry was loud and cheerful, ignorant of the fury clear in Ray's voice. "Surprise, surprise! What do we have here?"

Immediately, I thought Dogberry had seen Ray and I fucking in the kitchen. It wouldn't matter too much, because I knew Dogberry's time on this Earth was limited. But as I stepped through the kitchen's back door to round up Hannah, I heard a little girl's cough. It took me a second to realize, Dogberry wasn't talking about Ray and I.

Dogberry had found the girls. "Imagine my surprise when I caught these two hiding in our shed during my walkaround!"

I knew right then, all hell was about to break loose, but I didn't have a chance to turn around and rush to their aid, because a hand covered my mouth from behind.

EIGHTEEN

Ray

"**W**hat the actual hell?" I repeated. I couldn't see straight, because all I was seeing was red. Blood fucking red, and it was about to be Dogberry's fucking blood. The idiot had one of my sisters in each of his hands, gripping tightly to their arms. They looked absolutely terrified, each of them with their backpack strapped on.

I was proud of them, even at this moment. Even in their terror, they had remembered to save the supplies. But I would've given anything if they didn't have to act so adult-like at such a tender age.

"Shouldn't you be, like, excited about new girls?" Dogberry glared at me from behind his mask. Then he did a double take, looking between the girls and myself. "Oh, wait... These are your sisters!"

I wanted to punch him for the glee in his voice alone. My original plan had just been to knock him out and lock him in the basement, but now I was on a hunt for blood. "Take your filthy hands off of them. Immediately."

"Or what?" He grinned, showing way too many teeth. "You gonna run to your big brother Luke for protection? Last I heard, he wasn't too happy with you."

If I was certain I could get to my sisters before he could do anything to hurt them, I would've taken him down. But I couldn't be sure, and I couldn't risk it. I ground my teeth, trying to get a hold of my anger.

It was difficult with Avery looking at me like she expected me to save her, and Ella looking like she wanted to cry. "You don't know anything. How did you even find them?"

"Seems like I know more than you do." Dogberry shrugged. "And to answer your question, it was sheer luck. The gods must have been smiling on me today. There I was, doing my walk around, when I passed by the shed like I do every other time. Only this time, I heard a cough. And at first I thought I was hearing things, but then it happened again! So I open up the shed doors, and wham-bam-thank-you-ma'am, there they are!"

The gods were smiling on him all right, but only because I hadn't broken his neck yet. Ella looked up at me with tears in her eyes. "I'm sorry, Ray. I tried so hard not to cough!"

Dogberry frowned and shook her backpack, obviously irritated that his new pet was speaking. I was going to crush his skull with my bare hands. "Shut up," he snapped.

"Ella, it's okay. It's not your fault." I held up my hands, looking between the girls. I needed to deal with him, and quickly, before any of the other brothers showed up.

The only option I could think of was to appease him, catch him off guard, and hope the girls remembered this lesson in survival. I sighed.

"Look, man, I know we've gotten off on the wrong foot. But I just really want my sisters back. Send them my way, and we can forget this whole thing ever happened." I edged closer to the girls, trying not to startle Dogberry with any quick movements.

He tossed his head back and laughed. "Buddy, this goes way beyond you and me. You're an idiot if you think I'm holding onto these girls just to mess with you."

My blood ran cold, ice racing through my veins. "What exactly are you implying?"

"I'm not implying anything." Dogberry smirked. "I'm here to stall you until one of the other brothers finds your little girlfriend. I can't wait to see you choose between the three of them tonight. It's going to be the best entertainment we've had in weeks."

He couldn't be serious. I had just spoken to Luke yesterday, and everything seemed to be fine. Hadn't it? Unless even then, he had known more than he let on and was just toying with me, like a cat toyed with its dinner. I had been so confident, and now my carefully constructed plan was crumbling to pieces around me.

The girls stared at me, begging with their eyes. Ella silently wept, tears dripping off her face onto the floor.

I had promised my mom I would protect them, and I *would* protect them with my last breath. They would get away from this sick place, even if I couldn't. Shit, I hoped Mila had been able to hide before someone had caught her in the kitchen. If I was really lucky, she heard everything and hid.

I pushed my hood back, running my hands through my hair. "You're telling me Luke just happened to know I was bringing my sisters to the motel today? Seems a little far-fetched to me." I was grasping at straws, but there had to be some other explanation for this.

Someone wearing a pair of high heels clomped down the stairs behind me. I knew who it was before she said a word. Laura's voice taunted me.

"You really should learn to keep your voice down when you're fucking your girlfriend. You two were so caught up in your own bullshit you didn't even notice me listening outside your door. I heard your entire plan. Pathetic, really. You could've had it all. You could've had me, *Ray*."

I turned around, uncomfortable turning my back on Dogberry and my sisters, but in so much shock I didn't think twice. "You know my real name?"

Laura rolled her eyes, tossing her ratty hair over her shoulders. "Come on now. We all know the masks are a farce. I knew who you were the moment I walked into this building, of my own free will, I might mention."

I took a step backwards, closer to my sisters, but also encouraging Laura to keep her talking while I thought of a way out of this. "And Mila? What do you have against her?"

"Oh, Ray." She laughed, as if I had told the funniest joke in the world. "Don't you recognize me, baby? Because I remember you, from the first moment you walked in late to my English lecture."

I glanced back over my shoulder, checking on my sisters. They were still terrified, but thankfully Dogberry seemed too wrapped up in Laura's performance to be paying much attention to them.

All the while, Laura continued her monologue.

"You wouldn't remember me, though. You were so caught up in Mila the moment you sat down next to her." She gagged. "All semester, it made me sick. You and I, on the other hand, we could've made some *very* pretty babies that would've gone for some good money."

She was right about one thing. I couldn't tell you anyone else in that class because I only remembered Mila, and the vile professor. I shook my head, looking back and forth between Laura and my sisters.

"Look, I'm glad we've all cleared the air now, and I'm more than willing to admit I fucked up. But I'd really like for my sisters to go home now. You can do whatever you want with me as penance, but you need to let them go. Please." I always knew there might be a chance of this. I had prepared for it, prepared the girls for it too. But now that it was here, I realized it was going to be harder than I thought. "Just let them go."

I met Avery's gaze, and she mouthed something to me. I narrowed my eyes, watching her mouth more closely. *Mila.*

I nodded my head. *Yes. Find Mila.* They knew the plan.

But Avery frowned, shook her head, and looked over my shoulder. I turned around to see Tybalt dragging Mila into the room, kicking and protesting.

Not her too. I just needed to stay calm and in control of the situation. If I was lucky, I'd be able to get all three of them out safely. I didn't care what happened to me, as long as I could get them out.

Laura laughed once more. I never wanted to hear that sound ever again. "Oh, good, now we're all here. We just need to wait for Luke."

"Just sit the fuck down! God." Tybalt forced Mila into a chair. She twisted and spat at his feet. His face had a big scratch mark across it, red and raised. She was pissed, but I didn't feel sorry for Tybalt in the slightest. The dick deserved it, and then some.

I looked around the room. I could probably take one of them before they took me down, but that meant choosing between my sisters and Mila. An impossible choice. Would my sisters be able to survive without myself or Mila?

"I can hear your brain working from here, and no, sorry, there's no way out of this for you." Luke's voice cut through my thoughts. I balled my hands into fists. "God, I love the look on your face now that you realize what's happening."

I turned to glare at Luke, maskless but in his black hoodie. There was no room for games or make-believe anymore. We had been playing pretend since the beginning of the Collapse, and now that was over. "If you've known all along, why didn't you do something sooner?"

He shrugged, smirking. "More entertaining this way. Life has gotten pretty boring with the Collapse. I wanted to see how far you would take it, and apparently it was pretty damn far. I hadn't expected you to actually hide your sisters on site, so it was a delightful surprise Laura shared with me last night. And Hannah, pregnant! How wonderful for us. Too bad you won't be around to share in the bounty."

My nails dug into my palms. With or without me, my sisters and Mila were getting out of here, and then I was going to watch this place collapse to the ground.

"Don't worry, *Ray*. We'll take good care of your sisters for you. They'll be safe and sound here." Luke smiled at my sisters over my shoulders. My blood boiled under my skin. "Hannah will be tested and taken over to the pregnancy wing. And Mila, of course, will be available for choosing tonight. I'm sure Dogberry will be very, very gentle with her." Luke licked his lips and laughed.

No. No. No. This wasn't happening, not after so much careful planning. I looked out of the corner of my eyes, trying to figure out who I could take out first. Dogberry was closer, but if I could free Mila, she could help me get the girls out of here. I caught Mila's eye. She gave me the briefest of head shakes. *No.*

I knew what she was doing, because I was doing the same thing. Sacrificing herself for the innocent lives who still had a chance. My heart broke, but I knew what I needed to do. I sighed, looking up at Luke. "I understand. I failed the Kingsnakes. My own emotions got in the way, and I was a fool."

He nodded. "I appreciate your apology. Unfortunately, the transgressions you committed mean immediate dismissal."

Dismissal, otherwise known as death. Horror tied up in pretty packaging, just like everything else in this life. "What are you waiting for then?" I asked, throwing my arms out to the side. "Dismiss me now."

"That's not how we work, Ray." He laughed and gave me an indulgent smile. "Your brothers should be here soon. We'll deal with your dismissal together. I would take advantage of this time to say your goodbyes."

My goodbyes. I wasn't quite ready for that yet. And Luke was still watching me carefully. I needed to wait for my moment.

Laura sighed dramatically. "Shame, really. I was hoping to get my chance with him."

Tybalt spoke up for the first time since disciplining a still-glaring Mila. "Don't worry, sweetheart. You can still have me."

"Ugh, fine." I watched her shiver at the thought. "What are *they* doing here?"

We all followed her gaze up the stairs to where the rest of the girls stood huddled, watching the drama unfold. I couldn't say I blamed them. Luke turned his attention to them, scolding the girls as if they were children. But I needed to use this distraction. I ignored everyone and walked over to my sisters. I knelt down in front of them, wrapping them both in my arms, and bringing them as close to me as I could with Dogberry's tight grasp on them.

"I love you guys. You know the drill." I couldn't choke. Not now. I needed to get them safely out of the motel. We had practiced this scenario, this position before. They knew what to do.

"But, Ray," Avery whispered.

I shook my head. We didn't have the space for doubt. I had trained them in survival as much as education. They were more ready than they realized. I just hoped I was, too. "On my count," I whispered back. I glanced up at Dogberry, still distracted by Luke yelling at the girls. "One."

Avery looked unsure, her gray eyes wavering with emotion. But she still spoke the word. "Two."

I slowly made my way up from a crouch, giving Ella a nod. "Three," she whispered.

As I jumped to my feet, multiple things happened in rapid succession.

First, Luke demanded the girls come downstairs to be punished, creating a flood of people swarming into the common room.

Second, the rest of the brothers arrived at the front door, blocking my sisters' easiest exit to freedom.

And third, everyone froze when I snapped Dogberry's neck with an audible crack.

NINETEEN
Mila

So much happened at once, it was difficult to pinpoint the epicenter of chaos. All of a sudden, the common room was packed, and no one was paying attention to me.

Tybalt had been pushed away from my chair and was now hidden behind a crowd of girls. Kingsnakes were appearing out of nowhere, a swarm of black hoodies and bone masks. And when I looked up to find Ray, I expected to see him using the bedlam to usher his sisters to safety. Instead I watched him snap Dogberry's neck.

The sound startled everyone, and Dogberry dropped like a ton of bricks. Ray grabbed each of his sisters by the hand and pulled them to the front doors. But there were too many people, and too much commotion for them to reach the exit through the throng of people.

I shot up, shoving my way through girls and Snakes alike. Maybe if both of us pushed, we could get them through the door. Somewhere, Brutus was screaming for order.

Apparently he hadn't learned the crowd mentality rule – the one rule still valid post-Collapse. He had lost control the moment Ray killed Dogberry, judging by the screams of the girls who had seen it.

Ray looked panicked but relieved when I finally made it across the room. "We have to get them out of here!" he yelled.

I looked around the crowded room. A herd of black hoodies blocked the exit, still attempting to abide by Brutus's orders. There was no way we were getting out the door without some kind of distraction.

A *big* distraction. Ella brushed against my leg, reminding me of what was hidden there. My lucky lighter pressed against my thigh, and I immediately knew what I needed to do. Fire, the ultimate distraction.

I thought back to Brutus's office, lined with books and filled with newspapers, those tacky curtains still hanging on the window. I just needed to find something to make it burn *quicker*. And a tool to break in. I looked up at Ray. "I need you to trust me! Stay here!"

His eyes widened. "Where are you going?"

"To get us out of here!" I turned before he could stop me, wading back into the fray of bodies. How were there this many people in this room? It hadn't felt this crowded during my first Choosing. I focused on the kitchen door, my best hope for finding fuel and a tool, ignoring the people pushing and shoving all around me.

It wasn't that much further. I was almost there. Someone snatched my elbow, pulling me back just before I reached the kitchen door. I turned to look at a pair of furious blue eyes. Maybe I wouldn't have to break into his office after all.

"Where the hell do you think you're going?" Brutus roared in my ear. "You've been a fucking pain in my ass since day one."

I smiled at him, twisting my arm to gain some space between us. "Funny, you're just the person I wanted to see." I yelled back. I hadn't spent the last ten years twiddling my thumbs. Whenever I came to town, I grabbed old self-defense books from the decrepit library. I studied. Practiced.

Now that Brutus and I were one on one, I could do something about it. I looked back once more to check my aim, and elbowed him as hard as I could on the edge of his jaw. Maybe Olivia was with me at that moment, proud of the woman I had become.

Maybe she was why all of my strength propelled my upper body as I connected with his face. He dropped to his knees, looking up at me in surprise for a mere second before falling all the way to the floor.

"Asshole," I muttered, grabbing the set of keys off his belt loop. I didn't think I had hit him hard enough to kill him, but he wouldn't be a problem for the foreseeable future. I darted into the kitchen before anyone could stop me. Racing for the sink, I fell to my knees and searched for something that would work for my purposes.

There had to be something.

My hands dug through mouse traps, an ancient bottle of dish soap, and what looked like a dead squirrel.

And then there, behind the squirrel and the pipes, was a dusty bottle of rubbing alcohol. *Bingo*.

"Mila? What the hell is going on?" I whirled around to see a barefoot Hannah, sleep still scrawled across her face.

I had no idea how to explain everything that had happened. I looked down at the keys in my hand, the largest key that had "East" carved into its flat head. There was only one thing this key could be for. The East Wing where they kept the pregnant women.

We had to get those girls out too.

I jumped up, and twisted the large key off the ring. "It's a very long story, but I need you to take this key, and get the girls in the East Wing out of here. There shouldn't be any brothers on guard duty, because it's an absolute shit show in the common room right now."

Hannah took the key with a nod, seemingly unsurprised with the chaos she had stepped into. "Okay. What exactly are you planning on doing?"

"I'm going to burn this place to the ground." I embraced Hannah tightly, hugging the first friend I had known in a decade. "Be safe. Be quick. I'll see you on the outside."

"Thank you. For everything." She hugged me back, and then ran across the kitchen holding tightly to the key.

I watched her leave out the kitchen's back door. Then, bottle in hand, I raced for the common room again.

Lifting my elbows, I stuck to the walls to make it to Brutus's office as quickly as I could.

I hoped my fight with him hadn't lost me too much time, but I couldn't afford the precious seconds to check on Ray and the girls. I had to trust they were still waiting for me at the front entrance.

Finally I collapsed against Brutus's office door, elbowing a scrawny Kingsnake out of the way as I juggled the keys I had stolen. The door opened with the second key I tried, and I closed myself inside the small office – exactly how I remembered it.

The window was still there, draped in those horrendous polyester curtains. Stacks of newspapers, a wall of books, and the nasty-ass drapes begging to be torched.

Brutus had no idea he was hoarding the perfect catalyst for a house fire. I uncapped the bottle of rubbing alcohol, pouring it liberally over the curtains, moving on to the newspapers, and grimacing as the last of the liquid drizzled on the books. Bottle empty, I tossed it to the side, and took my lighter out of my pocket.

The light that seemed so useless on my own in the woods might now be my salvation. I struck a flame and held it to the edge of the curtain. It lit up immediately, sparking enough to catch the first stack of newspapers aflame. I didn't stick around to watch the books light up, but the crackling that followed me out the door told me it was a success.

Chaos still ensued in the common room, and it took me longer than I would've liked to get back to Ray and the girls.

Thankfully, they were right where I left them, the girls glaring at the row of Kingsnakes blocking the exit.

Neither party was making a move, and I was confused why the brothers weren't approaching him when they easily had him outnumbered. Then I saw the fury in his eyes – the determination to save his sisters. And me. Everything made sense. Ray grabbed my hand. "Well?"

I nodded. "Now we wait," I yelled. *And cross our fingers.* I grabbed the backpack off Avery's shoulders, hoping to relive her tiny frame of some weight.

It took less than two minutes for me to return, but it wasn't long before smoke was billowing into the common room. One of the girls screamed. "Is something on fire?"

I looked over the crowd. I could picture thick, black smoke was pouring out of the edges of Brutus's door, before the flames took over, inching out. I smiled in grim satisfaction. Apparently, the newspaper-covered wall didn't take long to burst into a raging inferno. The heat blew across the room in seconds. Everyone screamed. Ray looked at me. "What the hell did you do?"

"What I had to do!"

The fire was spreading along the walls quicker than I could've imagined, catching on newspaper and wallpaper alike. The whole motel became a huge tinderbox ready to burn. And as soon as the Kingsnakes guarding the door realized what was happening, they were the first to turn tail and run.

Which meant, our exit opened up. I grabbed Avery's hand, and Ray grabbed Ella's. The narrow hall filled with bodies trying to escape, smoke flooding the air. I couldn't see, and I could barely breathe, but I refused to let go of Avery's hand.

It only had to be a couple more feet. Just a few more. I followed the bodies, pushing our way out. Eventually, the smoke lessened, and a spark of daylight lit my path. A few more steps. *Just a couple more.*

And then we were outside. I sucked in a deep breath of clean air before turning and making sure everyone was still with me. Avery was still clinging to my hand. Ray was behind us, clutching Ella and herding us away from the quickly growing blaze. I scanned the crowd as we spread out, looking for one girl in particular. But I didn't see her red hair anywhere. I grabbed one of the girls as she ran past me, fear in her eyes. "Have you seen Hannah?"

She shook her head, and pulled her arm out of my grasp. "I haven't seen her since this morning at breakfast."

Fuck. Surely, she had gotten out safely. I had given her the keys and explicit instructions to get the pregnant women out, and more than enough time to get out of the motel. I couldn't have been the last to see her alive. *Could I?* I stopped, and turned to face Ray. All around us the fire crackled, wood snapping. Girls were screaming, trying to find one another. It was a mess. I cupped my hands around my mouth, pointing back at the motel. "Hannah!"

Ray frowned. "What?"

We didn't have time for this. "Hannah!" I screamed at him, trying to be heard over the mayhem. "Hannah is still inside! I gave her the key to get the pregnant women!"

We couldn't leave her, or any of the other women, behind. I started to shrug off the backpack, passing it back to Avery, but a hand stopped me.

215

"Take them to the forest!" Ray yelled. "I'll get Hannah and the rest of the girls!" He stuffed his watch into my hand, the watch he was never without, and I didn't want to think about what that meant.

"You promised," I whispered, knowing he wouldn't be able to hear me. I shook my head, trying to convince myself the wetness building in my eyes was from the smoke, not from the idea of leaving Ray behind. *Again*.

I should be the one to get her. I was the one who had started the fire. This was my mess to clean up. But Ray was already pulling the backpack back into place on my shoulders, yelling directions to his sisters. He kissed me hard on the lips. "Run, Mila!" he shouted. He turned and disappeared into the flames and smoke.

I couldn't do this again. I couldn't. My feet wouldn't move, but little hands pulled at me, tearing me away from the motel, into the boggy field that would lead us to the forest. My feet moved without my permission, tears pouring down my face. Smoke burned my eyes, and I was certain I had burns on my hands and legs from setting the curtains aflame.

Run, Mila. Olivia's voice in my head, begging me to escape and leave her behind.

Run, Mila. The girls I needed to protect ahead of me, screaming for me to keep up.

Run, Mila. Ray's broken command, a thousand unkept promises hidden in those two words.

Run, Mila!

So I did. I ran as fast as I could, keeping up with the girls, and hurrying us into the edges of the forest.

I knew we should keep going, to put as much distance between ourselves and the Kingsnakes as possible, but those assholes had bigger problems at the moment.

So once we ran into the treeline, I did what I hadn't done the first time I'd left town. I looked back.

"We should keep going," Avery whispered, tugging on my sleeve. Her heart-shaped face was so like Ray's, blonde curls framing gray eyes. In them, I could still see fragments of the innocent toddler I had spent my Saturdays with.

I shook my head and looked down at the watch he had thrust into my hand. "We're giving him five minutes."

Avery bit her lip, emotions warring across her face. "He told us not to wait for him."

"Ray says a lot of things. But he promised me we would leave together, so we're giving him five minutes. If we see anyone else come our way, we'll run, okay?"

Appeased, she turned back to Ella, rubbing her thin arms the same way I had comforted Hannah. I watched the burning building in the distance, small figures running every which way around it. I hoped they were the girls, getting the hell out while they could. I also knew I had done what I could for them, and now my priority was the two girls next to me.

One minute. The watch ticked past, the minute simultaneously taking hours and going by in a blink.

Two minutes. I sighed, rubbing the smoke out of my eyes. The wind was blowing the ash and debris toward the forest. Thankfully, the ground and trees were damp with the fall weather. The smoke was annoying, but didn't pose any danger.

Three minutes. Had I made a mistake?

Should I just take the girls and head for my camp?

We could collect my supplies and stay the night in the abandoned farmhouse, and decide what to do from there. My brain knew that was the right choice, but my heart wasn't ready to give up on Ray just yet. In all the chaos, time slowed down. All that remained in my bubble was the girls, the watch, and waiting for Ray. The only thing that mattered was the next 120 seconds. Even the forest seemed oddly quiet.

The crackling of the fire that seemed to fill my ears only minutes ago muddled to a quiet hush, whooshing past us. The now-silent breeze carried bits of burning paper, and I found myself wondering what books I had burned. What stories had I set on fire to save us all?

"Mila. We should go," Avery murmured. It suddenly felt like she was the adult and I was the petulant child, stamping my foot to get my way.

"He's got two more minutes. We can afford him that much." I stared at the fire blazing brightly, setting flame to every reminder of Kingsnakes there could be. His watch was ticking too fast, the seconds spinning by.

Come on, Ray.

Four minutes. "Mila?" Ella whispered next to me. "Ray will be okay, won't he?" It only took a moment for the rest of my life to flash before my eyes, Ray-less.

I didn't know if I could make it without him again, now that I knew what it felt like to be whole. And the girls... he was their entire world, and we were practically strangers.

Would they trust me?

I wasn't sure how well I could raise two innocent lives without him by my side. He needed to make it. I needed to see him racing out of the flames, telling us to wait.

The last few seconds felt like years as my hope dwindled to nothing.

Five minutes. I sighed, resolving myself to the fact that I needed to get his sisters away from the city. If he had sacrificed his life for us, then I needed to honor his last wishes. My survival instincts kicked in, even as my heart sank. Safety came first. Tears could come later.

"Okay. Let's go."

I tried to sound determined, stable for the girls' sake, but there was no mistaking the crack in my voice.

I'm doing this for you, Ray. All of it was always for you.

Taking one last glance at the smoky destruction behind me, I turned away. I was ready to lead my ragtag pack through the bushes when Ella gasped behind me. "He's coming!"

If hope had a taste, it was smoke and ash. If it was a sound, it was a collective holding of breath. I whirled around, squinting to follow her pointing fingers. It was hard to make out, but sure enough, there was a shaggy blond head of curls running our way. "Holy fuck."

"Language," Avery scolded. But even she couldn't help but smile, bouncing on her toes as Ray's figure grew closer and closer. I needed to remember to tell Ray he had done a great job raising her. Both of them.

He was ten feet away when I raced to meet him, leaping into his arms. "I didn't think you were coming."

Ray squeezed me tightly, and set me back on the ground. I took the moment to really look him over. His face was covered in soot, his blond curls gray with ash. He didn't look good, but he was *here*. Alive.

"I didn't think I was coming either. The smoke was so thick I couldn't see where I was going. I was able to crawl underneath it to find the doorway." He gave each of the girls a tight hug, and a kiss on their forehead.

"Hannah?" I asked. My chest was already tight with fear for my friend. If the smoke was that thick, would she have made it out okay? Would the pregnant ones?

"She got out with me. Last I saw she was running in the direction of her parents' place." He smiled at me, and I took a deep breath. "She'll be okay."

"And the brothers?" Avery asked with a grimace. Ella stuck her tongue out in agreement.

Apparently neither girl thought too highly of the Kingsnakes. I couldn't say I blamed them.

"Scattered. I'm sure some of them got trapped inside, but the ones who made it out were hightailing it back to the city. Funny how the toughest scare the easiest." I bit my lip. Ray took in my worried expression. "Hannah got them all out. They're safe, babydoll."

Relief washed over me. I had done what I could, but knowing they were safe made a world of difference. Knowing they could have their babies, and keep them, was even better.

Ray grabbed the backpack off Ella, and swung it onto his own back. "Come on. Even with the Kingsnakes down, we should cover serious ground before nightfall."

He set off into the forest, and like the Pied Piper, Avery and Ella trailed close on his heels. Those girls adored him. Ella's small voice piped up as they walked. "Can we go to the beach, Ray?"

"I don't see why not. It might take us a little while to get there though." Their conversation trailed off as they disappeared behind a tree.

I couldn't help but take one last look back at the blazing building against the backdrop of the sky. Turning away, the sound of Ella's sweet laughter caught my attention, and I was eager to catch up and hear the joke. I was leaving again, the city at my back. But this time, I was leaving of my own free will. This time, I wasn't alone.

This time, I had hope.

ALL ABOUT *Torri*

Torri Heat has always loved control. Her mind was blown when she discovered she could control entire worlds through story writing. Throw some steamy romance in there, and it was pretty close to perfection.

Torri loves dark heroes who ride off into the sunset on their motorcycles, fierce heroines who can fend for themselves, and a sprinkle of the paranormal to keep things interesting. When she's not creating alternate realities, you can find her managing her three-ring circus of kids and animals.

Find all of Torri's books and sign up for her newsletter at her website ww.torriheat.com, or follow her on social media @torriheat!

ALSO BY Torri

Watcher Series
The Ruins
The Reckoning
The Remains

Darkling Series
Nyctophilia
Caligo
Nighted
Cimmerian
Umbra

Standalones
Blood Crown
Nosedive
Jinxed (COMING SOON)
Gridlock (COMING SOON)

Printed in Great Britain
by Amazon

82187651R00131